"I've got to get to the bottom of this, which means . . ."

Sabrina contemplated the aquarium. "I've got to get to the bottom of *that!*"

She didn't know how to scuba dive. In fact, she wasn't all that good a swimmer. But thanks to witch magic, Sabrina came up with a perfect plan. Concentrating, she pointed her finger at herself.

The next thing Sabrina knew, she was inside a tiny bubble of air. Her bubble floated gently down through the aquarium water, down, down toward the castle on the underwater hill. Passing fish eyed her curiously.

A green blur flashed by. Then another. Looking up, Sabrina saw the merpeople she had freed from the uprooted plants. Then another flash of color caught her attention. From below came a murky gleam of gold, then another. A squad of armored mermen, each carrying a wickedly pointed trident, was swimming up to meet her.

Titles in SABRINA, THE TEENAGE WITCH™ Pocket Books series:

All Pocket Book titles are available by post from:
Simon & Schuster Cash Sales, P.O. Box 29, Douglas, Isle of Man IM99 1BQ
Credit cards accepted. Please telephone 01624 836000,
Fax 01624 670923, Internet http://www.bookpost.co.uk
or email: bookshop@enterprise.net for details

Sabrina The Teenage Witch™

Age of Aquariums

Bobbi JG Weiss and David Cody Weiss

Based on Characters Appearing in Archie Comics

And based upon the television series
Sabrina, The Teenage Witch
Created for television by Nell Scovell
Developed for television by Jonathan Schmock

POCKET BOOKS

LONDON · SYDNEY · NEW YORK

POCKET
B O O K S

An imprint of Simon & Schuster UK Ltd
Africa House, 64-78 Kingsway
London WC2B 6AH

Copyright © 1999 Viacom International Inc.
POCKET BOOKS and colophon are registered
trademarks of Simon & Schuster
A CIP catalogue record for this book is
available from the British Library

ISBN 0 671 02919 3

5 7 9 10 8 6

Printed by Omnia Books Limited, Glasgow

Chapter 1

☆

Sabrina Spellman fidgeted on the jouncing school bus seat, trying to find a comfortable spot. Like most public school equipment, the seats were showing their age—the padding was thin, and sharp springs lurked underneath it, ready to poke an unwary posterior. Appearances could be deceiving because spots that appeared to be smooth and unworn were often the most uncomfortable. *Not surprising,* Sabrina thought. *That's practically the definition of high school.*

It irked her how the simplest things could turn out to be minefields in disguise. For instance, being a teenage witch should make life simpler, not to mention a lot of fun. But since Sabrina had discovered on the morning of her sixteenth birthday that she was a witch—a half-witch, actually, since her mom was a mortal—magic had only complicated her life.

Since becoming a witch, Sabrina had learned about magical limitations, sometimes the hard way. Spells had to be constructed very carefully, she knew. A spell she had once cast to fix the school air-conditioning created a three-day snowstorm *inside* the school. Another careless conjuring had caused Sabrina's friends to tell the absolute truth—with disastrous consequences. In a nutshell, she had to hide her magical powers or they could lead to unexpected trouble—like this entire trip.

Sabrina heaved a sigh as she thought about the previous Friday when it had seemed perfectly reasonable to use magic as a shortcut. When Sabrina had gotten to school that day, she discovered two other girls wearing her exact same outfit. Magically changing clothes seemed like the obvious solution. One point of her finger and, presto, her outfit was changed and the fashion alert was over—except that Mr. Kraft, the vice-principal, had already seen her first outfit.

Not that he could tell what was different. Kraft was male, and males weren't born with the intensely discriminating fashion gene natural to females. All Kraft knew was that *something* about Sabrina was suddenly . . . *wrong* . . . and that meant he had to keep an eye on her.

Which was how Sabrina had found herself "volunteering" to be on the Mesmer Team, a group of students assigned to take that Monday morning off to pack up a collection of valuable books and artifacts from a mysterious mansion owned by the Westbridge millionaire recluse, Professor Austin Theobald Mesmer.

It wasn't all bad, of course. On the one hand, Sabrina was getting out of history and English to go on the trip. But on the other hand, losing class time meant that she'd have to catch up on the work later, probably costing her a weekend or her GPA. The good thing was offset by a bad thing, which in Sabrina's opinion made it all bad. Only low-quality bad, perhaps, but still bad.

On the other *other* hand, Mr. Kraft had promised that the Mesmer Team would earn extra credit, which would backstop her in case her grades got wobbly later in the semester. As a bonus, Harvey Kinkle was on the team as well— and sitting across the aisle from her. On the other other *other* hand, Libby Chessler was not only on the Mesmer Team, but she had, of course, appointed herself team captain, and was now sitting in the window seat next to Harvey.

Two more goods and two more bads. So far, they evened out. Still, the bad things seemed to outweigh the good. Sabrina sighed again. Either she needed to avoid using magic or she needed more hands to keep score of her good-bad tally.

Valerie Birckhead poked her arm. "It's me, isn't it?" She sat next to Sabrina looking as if the guilt of the entire world rested on her shoulders. "Okay, look, it's just that I have this terrible rash on my shoulder and I have to put this really *gross*-smelling ointment on it every morning. So

I put on some of my mom's perfume to cover it up. But it didn't work, so I put on some different perfume. And then, of course, the two perfumes clashed, but still they didn't get rid of the ointment smell, so I got one of those little deodorant things from my dad's car . . ." She paused, fishing out a green cardboard pine tree from under her shirt. "It was supposed to cover up the whole thing, but now you sniff anyway. It's not working, is it? And you're just too polite to tell me, right?"

Sabrina had assumed that the vile smell in the air was simply *eau de schoolbus.* She smiled at Valerie and cheerfully lied, "No. Really. I don't smell a thing." Then she leaned over to whisper to Harvey, "Do you think we should call the EPA?"

Harvey let his breath out in a whoosh. Sabrina hadn't noticed that he'd been holding it. When the red in his face faded, he asked in confusion, "Is smelling bad covered under the Equal Rights Amendment?"

"That's the E*R*A," butted in Libby. "And I, for one, am not in favor of it. I don't see why a woman should settle for mere equality when she's already naturally superior. Cheerleaders, anyway"—she smirked at Sabrina and Valerie—"not freaks. Especially smelly ones."

Before Sabrina could think of a comeback—a civil one, anyway—Vice-Principal Kraft stood up in the front seat. "Okay, people," he said

4

officiously. "Eyes front and center. Time to review your marching orders."

"When did we join the army?" a boy in the back whispered loudly.

"Heard that," snapped Kraft. He scrawled a name in his ever-present detention notebook. "You're lucky the school board won't let me institute a stockade or a firing squad. You're getting off easy with just a week of detention." His eyes swept through the small group before him. "Any other acts of insubordination? No? Good.

"As I was saying, I realize that you young people have all been raised on the junk-food culture promoted by network television programming and liberal parents, so you have no appreciation of what real money—money that's *inherited,* not earned—entitles one to. Therefore, when we get to the Mesmer estate, I ask that there be no gawking, no matter how sumptuous it is compared to your drab, middle-class homes. That means no touching and no drooling. No talking, either. Mansions are temples of affluence and deserve proper respect. Keep together, stay orderly, and merely limit yourselves to inhaling the aroma that permeates great wealth."

Kraft closed his eyes in anticipation of that pleasure and demonstrated an approving sniff. The sniff turned into an abrupt snort and his nose wrinkled in disgust. "What is that *stench?"* he demanded.

Valerie sunk lower into her seat. Sabrina jumped to her friend's defense. "Exhaust fumes?" She shrugged as Kraft turned a baleful eye her way. "You know how these old school buses are."

"It seems to be coming from your row," Kraft said suspiciously.

Valerie tried to blend in with the stained vinyl seat. Sabrina pointed down. "Big leak in the floorboards?"

"Well, open the window," Kraft snapped. "You may be content to die young, Miss Spellman, but I have other plans. My doctor says that my immune system is in a delicate transitional phase right now, and I'm avoiding all allergens and irritants. Except students, of course. I get paid to deal with you."

Valerie jumped to open the window, which was jammed with ancient gum and spitwads. To Libby's annoyance, Harvey left his seat and leaned over both Sabrina and Valerie to help. Sabrina felt a little tingle of appreciation. Any excuse to get close to Harvey was great. But the window still wouldn't budge.

Here was a classic example of the dilemma Sabrina always faced. If she limited herself to what mortals could do, she might as well just put a clothespin on her nose. If she wanted the window open, it was witchcraft time.

Sabrina thanked herself for wearing a long-sleeved shirt that day—what she called a "magic-friendly" shirt. Easily pulling her right hand back into the cuff, she flicked her hidden index finger at the window. A golden spark of magic flew from her fingertip to the window, and immediately the balky glass snapped upward. Mission accomplished.

Unfortunately, this miracle of physics caught Harvey in mid-tug. He lost his balance and landed flat across both girls' laps, his face smushed against the wall. Sabrina tried not to grin. "This seat is already taken," she quipped, "but in your case I'll make an exception."

Harvey turned his head and grinned back at her, but then the combination of *eau de schoolbus* and Valerie's amazingly revolting scent spoiled things. Harvey turned green and awkwardly scrambled back to his seat, only to have Libby, miffed that he'd deserted her, push past him and huff her way to the back of the bus. There, Desmond Jacobi, jock *extraodinaire,* was making life difficult for Gordie, nerd *ordinaire.* Dez and a bud were playing keep-away with Gordie's nasal spray bottle.

"But I need that!" Gordie moaned. "Otherwise I get all stuffed up!"

"Say what?" Dez asked, mimicking Gordie's nasal twang and tossing the bottle back over Gordie's head to Ray.

"Desmond Jacobi," Libby said sharply, "how could you be so rude?"

"Huh?" Dez grunted as he caught the spray bottle on the rebound.

Libby pouted. "You should have known that I

7

wanted to sit with you on this trip, but you didn't save me a seat!"

Dez turned to Gordie and growled, "Where's yer manners, geek? Don't you know you're supposed to stand up in the presence of a lady?"

Gordie looked terribly confused, but shambled to his feet, nodding to Libby. As soon as he was off the seat, Dez planted one of his Docs on Gordie's rear and pushed. The poor nerd went stumbling up the aisle.

Dez waved a hand at the empty spot. "Yer seat, mah-dam," he drawled.

Libby smiled sweetly at him and primly settled herself down. Dez studiously ignored her, busying himself with Gordie's nasal spray.

Sabrina had seen this whole exchange, and her magical trigger finger itched to teach Libby a lesson. But Harvey, thank goodness, stopped her by calling out, "Hey, Gordie, you can sit by me, okay?"

Gordie gratefully sheltered himself between Harvey and the window. "I need my spray, though," he complained, punctuating his words with a gurgling snuffle.

Harvey leaned out into the aisle and hollered to Dez, "Hey, man, why don'tcha be cool and give up the spray?"

Dez affected a cavalier tilt of his head. "And how does my coolness depend on that?"

Harvey shrugged good-naturedly. "Well, you don't want people thinking you're a jerk, do you?"

Dez snorted, as if at a private joke. He juggled the bottle in one hand, flipping it lazily end over end. "Well, I certainly wouldn't want my social standing to be jeopardized by Harvey Kinkle's poor opinion of me." He threw the bottle without warning. "Heads up!"

Harvey's football reflexes snapped into play, and he caught the bottle effortlessly. "Thanks . . . I think." He handed the bottle to Gordie, who uncapped it and applied it vigorously to each nostril, *spritz spritz!*

"Ahem," coughed Mr. Kraft. "If you young Heismann hopefuls are finished with practice, I'd like to finish my instructions to you, preferably before the millennium hits."

"Proceed, proceed," Dez said loftily.

Kraft made an instinctive grab for his pen, then decided that it wasn't worth it. He'd written the name Desmond Jacobi in his detention notebook so many times already—where was the threat? He simply sighed. "Now, we only have an hour this morning, so let us concentrate on recon and small-acquisition-retrieval maneuvers."

Harvey's brow furrowed in confusion. "Huh?"

Kraft snorted in exasperation. "That's military lingo for checking things out and bringing back small items. Don't they teach you *anything* in history nowadays? In any event, squad one— er, *team* one—will be responsible for removing items such as the encyclopedias, the maps, the butterfly collection, and of course, the million-matchstick model of the *Titanic*. Team two will supervise and work out a plan for moving the aquarium. Team two will be composed of Libby and Desmond, which means that all the rest of you will be on team one."

"I knew I was picked for the heavy lifting," muttered Harvey.

"I'm going to wind up with the butterflies, I know it," whined Valerie. "I mean, they're cute and all, but they're still bugs—too many legs! Ugh!"

Sabrina grumped at the division of labor. "Why do I get the feeling that the only exercise Libby gets today will be pointing her finger?" *As if hers could do anything special,* she added silently, flexing her own enchanted digit.

It was starting to look as if being on the Mesmer Team was going to be a drag.

Chapter 2

The bus climbed into the hills north of West-bridge, and Sabrina watched as the landscape changed. Brick buildings became clapboard ones. Tract homes gave way to wooded neighborhoods. Yards grew larger, and landscaping grew more and more lush. The ratio of man's work to Nature's shifted to a balance, then exploded in Nature's favor. Just a few miles from town the road snaked through thick stands of trees. Tucked away in these woods were the private estates of Westbridge's elite.

For two and a half centuries the noble, the wealthy, and the traders who'd founded the town had stashed their New World palaces in these hills. In Victorian times mill owners and shippers had worked to see who could build the most ostentatious dwelling. Now all of the palaces of that day were long gone, lost to fire, bankruptcy, or overaggressive antique hunters, leaving the Mesmer mansion the sole survivor of those robber baron homes.

A century of harsh New England frosts had destroyed Mesmer's orderly perimeter. Tall iron fence posts with knife-sharp tips leaned drunkenly along the roadside, and the bus barely missed getting scraped by a few of them. Then the vehicle passed a sign proclaiming HISTORICAL LANDMARK and turned into a wide drive that led up to the main building. Sabrina had her first glimpse of three stories of Victorian splendor. She half expected to see long-skirted ladies with parasols playing croquet on the lawn while handsome young gentleman fought for their honor. But the place appeared to be vacant except for a couple of gardeners.

And then, suddenly, Sabrina shivered.

This caught Kraft's attention. He stared at her suspiciously from under his shaggy blond brows. Since becoming vice-principal, Kraft had learned that if strange things happened, more often than not, Sabrina Spellman was nearby. He couldn't put a finger on why this was, but he was determined to keep an eye on the girl. She was hiding a secret, he was sure. He thought about the shiver. Was she sick and hiding it?

Across the aisle from Sabrina, Gordie took a healthy toot off his nasal spray, then froze, an expression of horror on his face. His cheeks reddened, his eyes squinted, and with explosive volume he fired off a volley of ear-popping sneezes.

Kraft whirled on the boy, thoughts of Sabrina shaken from his mind. "Did you come aboard this bus with a *cold,* mister?" he snapped.

Gordie seemed to be having difficulty regaining control. Sneezy aftershocks made him vibrate. "No, sir!" he snuffled. "I got allergies!" He looked down at his spray bottle with confusion. "But this is supposed to control my symptoms."

"I think a little more *self*-control would address the problem, young man. If you knew you were sick, you should have stayed home, out of concern for your classmates and *me.*"

"But I have a big science test this afternoon!" Gordie sniffled. "I have to take it!"

Kraft's expression hardened. "Education must not stand in the way of public health," he declared sternly. "Do you have any idea of the complex, *dangerous* anatomy of a sneeze? When you sneeze, globules of spit evaporate into the air, and the rest of us have to breathe that. Keep your globules to yourself, mister!"

Kraft whirled around and glared at the rest of the students, singling Sabrina out for a double-dose of eye daggers. "The next student I catch harboring infectious microbes on this mission will be quarantined for the duration!"

The vice-principal's threat was cut short by the squeal of brakes as the bus ground to a stop in front of the somber, frowning face of Mesmer Mansion.

By unanimous unspoken agreement, the very fragrant Valerie was the first student off the bus. By similar unofficial rules, everybody allowed Libby and Dez to saunter down the aisle next— jocks and cheerleaders have certain perks. As he passed her, Dez patted Sabrina on the head. "Season's greetings," he said with a smirk.

He'd left something on Sabrina's head. She reached up suspiciously and discovered a crumpled paper that proved to be a pepper packet from the cafeteria. *Talk about your basic kindergarten prank,* she thought, seriously questioning Dez's capacity for creative thought. She was tempted to show him what magic could do, but thought better of it. Kraft was already watching her, and there was no reason to make things worse.

Kraft led his team down a walkway between manicured lawns, past a line of budding rosebushes, and up to Mesmer's front door. He rang the bell, and the door opened a crack, revealing the face of a short, black-haired woman. "Good morning," Kraft greeted her. "I'm—"

"That Kraft fellow from the high school," she interrupted, not pleasantly. "I suppose you want to come in."

Kraft hesitated. "That would be my general preference, yes."

The woman opened the door wider and stepped aside. Kraft and the students filed past her, their footsteps echoing in the cavernous front hall. Light rainbowed through arched stained-glass windows, and silence blanketed the place like a dense snowfall. Linen drapes shrouded dozens of chairs, tables, desks, and sideboards. The foyer was easily as large as the school auditorium and seemed to be peopled with a convention of lumpy ghosts.

Everyone jumped as another voice shattered the quiet. "We're Mr. and Mrs. Coverano, the caretakers." The voice came from a square-faced man with dead-straight blond hair. He spoke with a slight southern accent.

"Pleased to meet you," said Kraft.

Mr. Coverano spoke slowly, as if choosing his words. "Look, we're not really sure about all this. We think—"

"We think that you're in too much of a hurry to pack up Mr. Mesmer's collections," his wife cut in. "He won't have been missing a full seven years until Sunday. We think you're jumping the gun."

"I agree with what she said," Mr. Coverano summed up.

Kraft held up a hand. "Excuse me, good people, but this isn't something any of us is qualified to discuss. The deal was negotiated by lawyers, and I'm sure that we all acknowlege that they know best." He waggled his fingers impatiently at them. "Now run along so my little laborers can do their work, hm?"

Mrs. Coverano turned on her heel and left, obviously displeased. Her husband followed more slowly, nodding his head as if coming to the gradual conclusion that Kraft made perfect sense.

As far as Mr. Kraft was concerned, of course, he did make perfect sense. He turned back to his students, his face alight with an expression Sabrina identified as suppressed greed.

"Oh, no, he's going to make a speech," Valerie whispered.

She was right. Kraft spread his arms wide. "This is an auspicious day, and you all should feel fortunate to share in it. This day will see a new dawning in the annals of Westbridge school administration. This day will witness the first acquisitions for Westbridge High School's new Augmented Studies Department, a new school project that I humbly hope will become the cornerstone of the Willard H. Kraft Learning Center!"

Gordie chose that moment to reapply his nasal spray. This time his reaction was worse than before. He spat out sneezes in machine-gun bursts, snapping Kraft out of his dream and drawing the vice-principal's fury like a lightning rod.

Sabrina flashed on the empty pepper packet and realized what Dez had done. He'd dumped pepper into Gordie's nasal spray! Even as a practical joke, that was going too far. Sabrina pursed her lips into a tight, thin line of anger. *Dez, you're going to regret that little stunt,* she decided, and pointed her index finger. Instantly

Gordie stopped sneezing and, with a flash of purple magic sparkles, his symptoms sparked into Dez, who picked up where Gordie had left off, sneezing off round after round. Holding back a satisfied grin, Sabrina pointed her finger at the jock once more, and Dez broke out in little spots.

If Kraft was alarmed at Gordie's threat to his health, he came near panic at the sight of Dez. "Y-you've got *spots!*" he blurted. Then his surprise gave way to outrage. "Mister Jacobi, you're under quarantine! March yourself right back to that bus and stay there until we're finished!"

Dez would have objected to his abrupt exile if he hadn't been staring in horror at his spots— between sneezes, that is. He stumbled from the room.

Kraft scanned the rest of the students with laser eyes, looking for a hint of flush, the slightest sniffle. He kept coming back to Sabrina and Gordie. But Sabrina was the portrait of innocence, and Gordie stood in a tranquil daze, having been transported to Nirvana when his allergies were banished.

Kraft wrenched himself back to the task at hand. He handed Libby a clipboard. "Here's the list of items we're taking today, and the projects we need to estimate, Miss Chessler. Make your assignments as you see fit."

Libby accepted the clipboard with a sour smile. She'd been planning on spending her time with Dez, admiring how good they looked together in these grand settings. Now with Dez exiled to the bus, she was miffed and ready to take it out on someone.

Her eyes flicked down the list, sorting jobs by unpleasantness. She glared at Gordie. "You're first, Gordie. You get to pack the library. It's very dusty, I understand."

Gordie's eyes almost swelled up at the threat of another intense allergen immersion. Libby smiled sweetly, handed him a job slip, and then, as if he'd been a stain easily wiped clean, she forgot him, turning herself full-gear into manager mode.

The way Libby played the management game was to apportion jobs according to two criteria: by the social status of the student or by what self-debasement and flattery the student offered as a bribe. She read out job categories and then mused aloud about the kind of person each needed. She made the students compete with each other before making her choices. She inevitably gave each student the job he or she wanted the least.

That was true Power, and Libby Chessler knew how to wield it.

Left to the very last, Valerie and Sabrina stood restlessly in front of Libby, waiting for the hammer to fall. Libby milked the moment.

"I really wanted to make sure the two of you got jobs that suited you," she purred. "Valerie, you get to catalog the entomology collection. You'll love it. And for you, Sabrina, there's a miniature aquarium that you have to figure out how to move. You'll work together in the museum wing. That's where Mesmer kept his *freak* collection." She smiled coyly. "You two should complete the set."

As Libby walked away, Valerie wrinkled her lip in disgust. "Entomology—that's bugs, isn't it?" She moaned in despair. "I knew it, I knew it, I *knew* it!"

"I'd trade you for my miniature aquarium," Sabrina offered. "But knowing Libby, it's probably worse. Tiny, but gross."

Sabrina peered at the blurry copy of the house diagram that came with her job slip. "It looks like the museum wing is on the far side of the house, a floor down. Come on."

The two girls went downstairs and then through a side room, emerging into a hallway that opened on the wing where Professor Austin Theobald Mesmer kept his odd collections. Their footsteps were muffled by deep oriental carpets. Dark polished mahogany and teak paneling made the hallway feel tunnel-like. Lining one wall of the hall were portraits, presumably of former Mesmers, each identified by a Roman numeral. The era of each ancestor could be easily identified by the clothing worn by the sitter. The present-day Augustus resembled his forebears—they could all have been brothers, except for their costumes.

"This is sooo creepy," said Valerie as she

passed each portrait. "I'd get paranoid if I thought my whole family was watching me like this."

"I don't know," said Sabrina. "I think it's kinda cool to know what your ancestors really looked like. These paintings are family treasures."

"Somehow, I don't think a portrait of Mesmer in a powder blue leisure suit playing PONG will be anything to treasure," Valerie said.

"And what's wrong with leisure suits?" Vice-Principal Kraft stepped unexpectedly into the hallway. "I still have three at home. It's only a matter of time before they come back into style."

"Actually," Sabrina said, charging to Valerie's defense, "we were worried that the blue color would fade over time. You know, like how my aunt Zelda's photos from the sixties have yellowed with age."

Kraft eyed her. "Not a chance, Miss Spellman. Mesmer always bought the best. The whole family did. If you paid attention in school, you'd know your local history better." Obviously Kraft greatly admired the Mesmer family. "They were true American entrepreneurs, even before there was an America," he stated. "They were major importers and shippers by colonial times. They didn't import coffee or tea, oh, no, they went straight for the hard-core stuff—*chocolate.* They cornered the cocoa market and never let go of it.

During the Chocolate Embargoes of the Mexican Wars—quick, the date . . . ?"

What is this, a pop quiz? Sabrina asked herself. "Uhh . . ."

"1846!" Kraft snapped. "It was a Spanish-controlled product, remember. Anyway, the Mesmers didn't let a little thing like *war* get in their way. The Augustus at that time smuggled barrels of syrup into the country to make a killing in the Ohio Territory. Wealthy men—unstoppable men! That's why I know that portrait accurately shows the pinnacle of fashion at that time." He drew in a deep breath, as if savoring a glow from the Mesmer tradition. Then he gestured to a set of double doors. "Your aquarium is right through there, Sabrina. Valerie, your bugs are this way."

Valerie grimaced as the vice-principal steered her down the hall. Sabrina suppressed a smile and, throwing open the double doors of the aquarium suite, beheld her charge.

She blinked twice and her jaw dropped. "M-Mr. Kraft?" The vice-principal was already gone. Sabrina was alone with her problem. A very big problem.

Chapter 3

☆

☆

The aquarium room of the museum wing was nearly the size of the school gym. Glass cases lined the walls with a wide assortment of flat-eyed fish-mummies staring blindly out—some were modern species, others fossils of long-dead ancestors. Even odder undersea creatures floated motionlessly in formaldehyde-filled jars on shelves below the display cases. A great stuffed hammerhead shark hung on one wall, and on the opposite wall hung an equally enormous stuffed swordfish. The entire room was a marine morgue.

Amidst these displays sat the main attraction—the aquarium. Larger than a king-size bed and mounted on a yard-high pedestal, the squar-ish tank hulked in the center of the room, its watery depths lit by an array of specially rigged lamps. Instead of guppies, goldfish, or the usual tropical fish, however, everything in this tank was a tiny or dwarfed version of a larger species.

Oh, thought Sabrina, *it's* that *kind of miniature.*

The bottom of the tank had been carefully designed to resemble an ocean bottom—in lilliputian scale. The stones and sand of the seafloor were nearly microscopic. Itty-bitty kelp clumped on the edge of a sculpted canyon and threaded its way toward the surface. Sharks no longer than Sabrina's little finger lurked in the shadows, and a pod of hand-size whales sported in the deepest corners.

The centerpiece was a small hill—or mountain, at that scale—that rose up from the center of the tank. Someone had gone to great trouble to create the illusion of a pastoral island, only underwater. The mini-mountain wouldn't have looked out of place in the Mediterranean Sea of old, if one could ignore the fact that the "grass" was some kind of moss, and that the trees and bushes all swayed in fluid instead of air. Tiny paths wound around the greenery, connecting little villas with an elaborate model city sprawling over the mountaintop, all done in a sort of ancient-Greek style architecture. It was impressive—stunning, really—but the massive tank with its miniature contents left Sabrina with a giant-size problem.

"How am I supposed to move this?" she moaned in disbelief.

"Do you always give up before you begin, Miss Spellman?"

Mr. Kraft's unexpected comment made Sabrina nearly jump to the ceiling. She whirled around to face the vice-principal as he strolled into the room. "Why do you keep *doing* that?" she demanded.

Kraft looked smug. "It's an old teacher trick— keeps students on their toes. In answer to your question, *you* aren't supposed to move the aquarium. You're supposed to take notes on it, then call around for estimates."

"Isn't that a little beyond the average high school assignment?"

Mr. Kraft examined his fingernails, a move calculated to convey a sense of casual menace. "Nonsense," he said. "Consider it preparation for life. In fact, consider it a substantial part of your economics grade."

"What?" Sabrina squealed. "That's not fair! This wasn't listed in the class syllabus!"

"Life isn't fair, Miss Spellman. If it were, I'd be a vice-regent instead of a vice-principal and I'd still have all my hair." At the sight of Sabrina's expression, Kraft softened. "I really shouldn't do your work for you, but I'll give you some tips. What you have to do is get some estimates. Call some hauling companies about moving the tank. Then, figure out how many fish you have to move and calculate the number of plastic containers you'll need to put them in—"

Sabrina was surprised. "You mean those plastic thingies that people put leftovers in?"

"Yes," Kraft said, pursing his lips. "They'd be perfect for the fish. Here's a brochure." From out of his pocket he pulled a glossy, tri-fold pamphlet and handed it to her. "Decide how many you'll need of each kind, then give me the total so I can order them in time for the move."

"Wait, so that *you* can order them . . . ?" Sabrina was sensing a trend here.

Kraft flashed his best plastic sales smile at her. "Westbridge High School is fortunate that I'm the local distributor for these plastic houseware products. I can supply all their storage needs at a substantial discount."

"Mr. Kraft, isn't your selling things to the school kind of a conflict of interest?"

Kraft waggled his hand in a "puh-leeeeze" gesture. "Nonsense. Do you know what a school administrator gets paid nowadays, Miss Spellman? It's a disgrace. In fact, if it weren't for my devotion to the cause of higher education, I'd give *all* my time to my plastic housewares franchise. It's the ultimate opportunity to create wealth while controlling your own destiny. Which reminds me"—he took a step closer and said with grave interest—"have you considered your future? Where do you expect to be in five years?"

"Uh—in college?" Sabrina couldn't believe that the vice-principal was actually slipping into a recruitment pitch. She recognized the symptoms because her aunt Hilda had once gotten hooked on peddling HomeHex premixed spell packs. As a result, all their witch friends had avoided the Spellman house for six months, and the basement was still jammed with boxes of Cup-O-Potion, Flab-Away, and Gnome-Away-From-Home Sprite Repellent.

Sabrina returned Kraft's smile with an equally insincere one. "Call me old-fashioned, but I think I'd rather get my degree before devoting my life to a marketing scheme."

Kraft shrugged. "Suit yourself. But think about it when you're an undergrad living on boiled noodles and slaving away on a truly original thesis paper that your professor will take credit for anyway."

"Yeah. Right." Sabrina tried to steer the conversation back to some kind of coherent point. "So where on campus am I supposed to park the aquarium? Aren't we already so short of class space that your secretary is working out of a broom closet?"

"I've solved that problem," said Kraft. "You can put it in the old maintenance building."

Sabrina visualized the school grounds. "We don't have an *old* maintenance building, just *a* maintenance building."

"Yes, well," said Kraft, "I'm dividing it into two separate facilities. The maintenance staff will move to the rear section. The plastic containers I sell have Cubicles, which allows them to interconnect with side-to-side locks. And they're stackable."

"Is *that* what those are!" Sabrina remembered seeing rows of weird rectangular boxes outside the maintenance building. "I thought those were portable potties for the football games."

A stunned expression crossed Kraft's face. "What a wonderful idea," he muttered. He pulled his detention notepad out of his pocket and began scribbling notes as he hurriedly left the room. "If I can get this suggestion to my franchise manager, he will *have* to pay me a bonus!"

He was gone in a flash, leaving Sabrina alone with the improbable fish tank and her impossible task. How was she going to get this thing moved?

☆

Chapter 4

☆

"Aunt Hilda! Aunt Zelda!"

Sabrina materialized in the living room of the Spellman house wound as tight as a spring. She had been fretting about how to move the fish tank through all of her afternoon classes, and now she was so anxious to find a quick solution to the problem that she had taken the unusual step of zapping herself home as soon as school had ended.

She found her older aunt, Zelda, sitting primly on the piano bench. Zelda wasn't playing the instrument, however, but was reading a scientific journal propped up on the music stand. Sabrina's younger aunt, Hilda, lay sprawled on the couch watching the events listings on the Home Witching Network. The titles of that evening's Other Realm TV shows were gradually scrolling down the screen: the perennially favorite sitcom,

My Mother the Frog at six o'clock; *Pointing Etiquette* at six thirty; *Baywitch* at seven; and *Hex Files* reruns at eight.

Sabrina cleared her throat. "Aunt Zelda, Aunt Hilda, I have a problem." They didn't respond. "Look, I really need your help!"

"Do you hear a wheel squeaking again?" Hilda asked, not looking away from the TV.

"Distinctly," replied Zelda, turning a page in her journal. "Is it time to apply the oil?"

Hilda nodded. "One social lubricant coming right up." She flipped her hand palm-up and a small vial appeared. A finger-flick by her other hand levitated the vial across the room to hover over Sabrina.

Zelda finally looked up from her book. "We're sorry to have to do this to you, sweetheart, but you've been getting too dependent on our help," she told Sabrina sternly but with some sympathy as well. "You have to learn to figure things out for yourself, so——"

"We're tuning you out with Oil of Oblivion," Hilda finished bluntly. Patience was not her strong suit.

After six hundred-odd years of being siblings, Zelda was used to Hilda's in-your-face style. Without missing a beat she continued, "We won't be able to hear a thing you ask us about magic. That way you'll learn to rely on your own resources."

"And we'll get a vacation without leaving

home." Besides being impatient, Hilda liked to get in the last word.

With one snap of Hilda's fingers, the vial over Sabrina flipped upside down and a drop of blacklight purple liquid plopped onto her head. "Eww! Wait a minute—!" Sabrina began, but Zelda was already murmuring a spell.

The little blob of oil tingled on Sabrina's scalp and seemed to seep through her skull, right through her brain and down to her throat, where it settled against her larynx. She opened her mouth to yelp, but nothing came out.

Then her voice returned. "Hey!" she yelled. "That's not fair!" But the words came out as less than a whisper.

"Oil of Oblivion also muffles complaints," added Hilda cheerily. "It's really a great product."

Clearly Sabrina wasn't going to get sympathy from this crowd, so with a whispery growl, she whirled around and stomped upstairs to her bedroom to sulk. When she threw herself down on her bed, a petulant yowl sounded from under it.

Sabrina rolled onto her stomach and peered under the bed. A black American shorthair gave her an upside-down glare. "Watch it, willya? There's a cat trying to take an afternoon-tuna-snack-nap under here," Salem said.

Technically, he was a cat. For the time being, anyway. Salem had been a young male witch until he'd been caught plotting to take over the world. For that crime, the Witches' Council had sentenced him to a hundred years in the form of a feline.

"Don't talk to me about stupid fish," Sabrina groused at him.

"I like stupid fish," Salem said. "They're the easiest ones to catch. Why are you complaining about fish?" His golden eyes grew big and round. "Do you have a present for me? A surprise present? Yum-yum! Bring 'em on!" Salem's human characteristics had a hard time outweighing his cat-body instincts. In the case of food, they never had a chance—the stinkier the food, the more Salem seemed to like it.

But Salem's enthusiasm only served as the final straw for Sabrina. "They'renotforyouthey're inastupidfishtankthatI'vegottamoveandmyaunts won't HELP me!" she shouted in a rush.

"Gesundheit," replied Salem.

Sabrina rolled onto her back on top of the bed, moaning, "Everybody wants me to work stuff out on my own." When Salem scuttled out from under the bed and joined her on the covers, she pleaded, "Salem, will you help me figure out how to do this by myself?"

"If I help you figure it out, then you won't be doing it by yourself."

"Salem!"

"Okay, okay, if there are fish involved, count me in." He flexed his claws into the blanket a moment and kneaded one little spot. Then he circled the area once and sat down. "First," he said, settling himself comfortably, "take stock of your assets."

Sabrina sat up and ticked points off on her fingers. "I'm in trouble, I'm desperate, and you're going to help me."

Salem yawned. "All this angst over a few little guppies?"

"They're not guppies," said Sabrina, "they're like toy fish in a 3-D stage. It's weird. Anyway, Kraft wants me to figure out how to move the whole aquarium—for school credit, no less!" She threw herself back on the pillows and covered her eyes with her hands. "I'm gonna flunk out and be doomed to a life of zapping up burgers and asking, 'You want flavor in that?' "

Salem gave a little tilt of his head—a cat version of a shrug. "Hey, I've got it. Make nice to the wrestling team and they'll carry it for you. Never underestimate the power of flirting."

"Who do you think I am—Libby? The jock-types at my school don't even know I'm alive. Besides, this aquarium is too big for that. It's like an indoor fishpond."

Salem smiled, his sharp fangs turning what should have been a pleasing expression into an unnerving carnivore leer. "What a wonderful idea! Like having a snack bar in your own home! Now, *that* I'd like to see."

Sabrina brightened. Her eyes twinkling with sudden mischief, she flicked a finger and sent a spiral of magical spangles racing around Salem's body. The spangles expanded to include her, too, and with a flash, her bedroom had vanished and she was standing in a hallway somewhere inside Mesmer's mansion.

Salem blinked, surprised to find himself curled up on a plush oriental carpet instead of on Sabrina's comforter. "Next time don't take me literally," he drawled, rising to his feet. "Oooh, but I must admit this feels wonderful." He started to flex his claws in the carpet, his purrs growing loud, when Sabrina cut him off.

"I must have gotten turned around. I think the aquarium suite is this way." Turning on her heel, she started down the hallway that she and Valerie had taken that morning.

The mansion was darker now that the Coveranos had gone home for the day and turned out all the lights. Enough late-afternoon sunlight filtered through the windows to guide Sabrina to a set of big double doors. "It's in here," she said, and stepped through.

A huge brown bear reared over her head, its enormous platter-size paws ready to grab, its finger-long fangs ready to rip and tear. Sabrina yelped in terror.

Salem chuckled. "If he's the fish you've got to move, I see your problem."

Sabrina struggled to calm herself. "Wrong room," she managed to say, and, turning her back on the stuffed grizzly, led the way to another door farther down the hall. "This is the one." She opened it and gestured. "This time, after *you.*"

With supreme cat coolness, Salem trotted confidently into the room. Then he stopped dead in his tracks and gasped.

Sabrina's adrenaline level had just about returned to normal, but now it shot up again, and her heart thudded. "What's the matter?" She bolted through the doorway. "What is it, Salem? Salem!"

Salem stood gawking at the huge aquarium towering before him. Undulating shapes glided to and fro within its oceanic depths, and smaller forms zipped about in sudden spurts, following close together like pearls on a chain. A sudden flash of iridescent scales revealed the larger fish, floating among the lush aquatic vegetation, their lidless eyes open and glassy.

Salem trembled. "Oh yyyeeessssss!" One leap and he was on top of the tank, his paw down an opening meant for filtration tubes. "C'mon, ya little fry, come to poppa!" he urged, thrashing at the water. Startled surface swimmers scattered down to safer depths.

"Salem!" All thoughts of boogeymen lost, Sabrina rushed to the aquarium and grabbed the cat. "This is not a private sushi tank!"

"I can't help it," Salem whined. "They're moving around."

Sabrina set him on the floor. "Yes, fish tend to do that. Just remember, you're allowed to eat the canned kind, but if it still has fins and wriggles—paws off."

Unable to stop himself, Salem leaped back onto the aquarium and thrust his furry arm down into the water again. "But look at 'em, Sabrina!" he panted, batting around. "They're better than my catnip mousie toy! And they smell *soooo* good! I bet they taste even better."

This time when Sabrina picked him up, Salem struggled. He howled frantically, "I can't help it! It's my instinct!" Then he calmed himself and stared her straight in the eye. "Do you think *we* could get an aquarium?"

"Right after we move this one." With that, Sabrina dropped him. Salem landed soundlessly on all fours with an undignified grunt. "So, got any ideas, cat?"

Miffed at having his fun spoiled, Salem leisurely licked a shoulder. "Just the usual—use magic."

"I can't."

"Why not?"

"Salem, I'm supposed to solve mortal problems with mortal ways. Don't you think Mr. Kraft would notice if the tank just *appeared* at school?"

"If it didn't cost him anything? Not at all. That's the great thing about mortals. They'll accept any explanation, no matter how lame, because their mundane little brains simply can't accept the fact that magic is real—and worse, that they don't have any."

Sabrina thought about it. "You could be right. Mr. Kraft has already swallowed some real whoppers I've told him." She brought her hand up, her pointing finger ready. "Okay then, do you think I should move the fish separately, or move everything at once?"

"I'm not the guy to ask. As a kid, I had a terrible tragedy with a bowl of guppies when I changed their water. Ever since then, I feel unqualified to take care of fish. I just eat them."

"I'll take that as a vote for moving the whole setup at once, including the water. Here goes." Sabrina pointed her finger at the massive aquarium.

"Hold it!" Salem said sharply. "Don't you think you'd first better make sure that nobody's around the maintenance building?"

"Oops. You're right. There are always workers on campus after hours." Sabrina thought a moment. "One Looky-Loop coming up!"

Sabrina took her already-pointed finger and rotated it in a large circle, murmuring a spell under her breath. A luminous disk the size of the circle appeared in midair, flickered for a second, then dissolved into a view of the interior of the maintenance building at Westbridge High School.

Sabrina made the Looky-Loop swivel around to display the entire space available. Satisfied that any employees were either somewhere else on campus or snug in their own homes, she invoked a transportation spell. In an instant, she, Salem, the aquarium, its podium, the castle, and all the little fish were magically shifted to the maintenance building some seven miles away.

Sabrina surveyed the tank in its new setting. She had placed it away from the center of the room, but with enough space so that people could walk around it. "So much for that problem," she said smugly. "This ought to leave Mr. Kraft in awe of my resourcefulness."

"Maybe you should check on the fish now," Salem suggested. "Of course, I'll be happy to do it for you. . . ."

"No, no," Sabrina said quickly. "I can do it without having to digest them. But thanks for the offer."

Sabrina knew that the underlying spell technology of the Looky-Loop allowed for more than just long-distance observation. At its most basic, the Looky-Loop was a magical device that first amplified distant phenomenon, allowing one to view distant locales, but a witch could also use a Looky-Loop to amplify "inner space," the realm of thought.

Sabrina floated the Looky-Loop to a position between herself and the aquarium. Then she peered through it, narrowing her concentration to one fish, a little roundish one with bulgy eyes and strange prickles all over it. Her concentration narrowed more and more as she eavesdropped on its thoughts.

First, she lost awareness of herself as a human, becoming instead a flicker of movement through the water. All sensation in her world became tuned to changes in pressure, current, and shafts of filtered light. Slowly fish thoughts formed in her mind. *"Food. Eat. Swim. Breathe. Food. Food. Swim. Breathe. Food."* When she caught her mouth opening and closing in time with the fish thoughts, her cheeks puffing in and out like mini-balloons, Sabrina shook her head and snapped out of the spell.

"That was attractive," Salem drawled. "In fact, I think that puffer fish likes you."

Sabrina opened her mouth to retort, then thought better of it. The fact was, the little puffer fish really did seem to be watching her with intent interest. "You're cute, too," she told it, then circled the tank, examining it.

Satisfied that the fish were happy and that things were under control, Sabrina scooped Salem up from the corner where he'd gone to sniff for mice. "This turned out pretty well, don't you think?" she asked the cat. "And for once, you even helped. It never would have occurred to me that changing tank water could hurt fish."

"It does if you change it into fruit juice, like I did," the cat said.

Just for that, Sabrina zapped herself back to her bedroom, but made sure that Salem wound up in the backyard.

Chapter 5

☆

Relieved that her aquarium dilemma was solved, Sabrina went downstairs to discover the Spellman house empty. A handwritten note was pinned to the refrigerator:

Dear Sabrina,
 Popped to Fukuoka for a Mendelssohn concert. Should be back late tonight—or tomorrow—we think. Zap yourself something nutritious for dinner—NO chocolate-covered toaster treats.

 Love,
 Zelda and Hilda

"Fukuoka?" muttered Sabrina. She zapped a world atlas into her hands. "That's in Japan!" she said, seeing that Fukuoka was just across the Sea of Japan from South Korea.

Well, world-hopping in pursuit of entertainment was one of the perks of being a witch. Sabrina really wasn't all that surprised, except that her aunts usually tried to make her attend cultural events with them. "Culture is food for the soul," Zelda would say. To which Hilda would add, "And you can meet cute guys."

Sabrina made herself a sandwich, did some homework, then settled down to watch TV. She wondered what time it was in the Land of the Rising Sun. All that did was give her a headache—she could never remember if you lost a day or gained one when crossing the international date line. She finally decided that, regardless of the time, her aunts were no doubt having a Mendelssohnian blast.

Then another thought nagged at her. Was the aquarium okay? "Of course it is," she lectured herself. "You zapped everything to school in one lump, and you checked it over yourself. What could possibly be wrong? It's all there, just the way it was at Mesmer's estate."

Still, something bothered her, so much so that she finally had to turn the TV off. "Oh, I suppose one last look wouldn't hurt."

After slipping on her sandals, Sabrina quickly zapped herself back to the Westbridge High maintenance building. There sat the enormous aquarium, as tranquil as ever. The sun had set, so the aquarium was wrapped in shadows now, its innermost depths black and silent.

"Looks good to me," Sabrina muttered, walking all the way around the tank, examining it closely. What fish she could see hung in the water like little floating toys, lazily flicking a fin now and then, just enough to keep them upright in their sleep. All the aquatic plants were in their proper places, and the Greek model city on the mini-mountain looked as peaceful as a real city asleep.

But something was wrong. Sabrina *knew* that something was wrong. "Okay, what?" she finally demanded of the tank itself. "What's wrong? What did I forget?"

The aquarium, of course, said nothing.

"Oh, fine, make *me* figure it out." With an annoyed grunt, Sabrina zapped herself back home to the kitchen. "Salem! Where are you?"

"Outside where you left me," came a voice beyond the back door. Sabrina let the cat in, asking, "So why didn't you just use the kitty door?"

"I know when I've been snubbed," Salem replied.

"Well, I'm glad you're here now, because I need your help."

"Oh, fine," Salem groused. "Dump me outside, then beg for favors."

"I learned the technique from you," Sabrina pointed out. "Here's the thing—I went back to school to check on the aquarium—and something's wrong."

"So fix it."

"I don't know what it is."

Salem leaped up to the countertop. "In the words of the immortal Bard, 'Aye, there's the rub.'"

"But it's just a feeling," Sabrina admitted. "I mean, I don't know anything about aquariums, but I have a horrible feeling I've done something wrong and if the fish die Mr. Kraft will kill me because this isn't just any tank, it's Mesmer's and—"

"All right, calm down," Salem interrupted. "There's an easy solution to the problem. If you don't know anything about fish, just ask somebody who does."

Sabrina grinned. "Of course. I knew that." She raised her index finger. "Come on."

Two seconds later cat and girl stood outside the local Claws 'n' Jaws Pet Mart and Aquarium Center. It was closed.

Salem gazed up at the storefront, with its colorful painted advertisement: FREE KITTEN WITH $10 PURCHASE! "I resent that," he muttered.

"It's closed?" Sabrina peered through the glass doors and into the dark, empty store, realizing with a weird little stab of déjà vu that the murky depths of Claws 'n' Jaws reminded her of the murky depths of Mesmer's aquarium. "How can they be closed when I have a problem? Now what do I do?"

"Take me back home?" suggested Salem.

With no other choice, Sabrina did just that. When she and Salem reappeared in the Spellman kitchen, however, it was no longer empty. Zelda was sitting at the table working on the newspaper crossword puzzle while strains of a sweeping violin solo wafted in from the adjoining dining room.

"Aunt Zelda, what are you doing here?" Sabrina asked. "Aren't you supposed to be in Japan?"

Zelda looked up. "Oh, hello, Sabrina. Yes, we were in Japan, but thanks to Hilda, we're back early."

Hilda's head popped through the dining room doors. "The concert was awful," she said, "and I said so to the conductor. In fact, I told him the first chair violinist didn't know the second movement of Mendelssohn's Violin Concerto in E minor from Flatt and Scruggs's theme to *The Beverly Hillbillies.*"

"And they threw you out?" Salem asked.

"Nope. The conductor invited me to put my money where my mouth was." Hilda grinned. "I've got an audition with him tomorrow!"

"Don't worry, I put some Oil of Oblivion on her violin," Zelda explained to Sabrina. "Even if she plays it all night, you won't hear a thing."

"Great." Sabrina paused. "Uh, look, before you two go back to puzzles and practice, I have a teensy little problem—"

"About magic?" Zelda asked sharply.

Sabrina gave a nervous little laugh. "Sort of. Well, not really. You see—" She stopped. Her voice was gone!

Hilda smiled and withdrew into the dining room to practice her violin. Zelda turned back to her crossword puzzle.

"Now wait a minute, this isn't fair!" Sabrina shouted. "Oops! My voice is back again."

"You can talk as long as you don't ask for advice on solving your problems," said Zelda amiably, filling in some squares on her puzzle. "We told you before, Sabrina, you've got to learn to rely on your own resources."

"But it's only one little question about—" Her voice cut out again.

Salem snickered. "I gotta remember this one next time I'm called before the Witches' Council."

"You be quiet, cat," Sabrina snarled at him, and stomped upstairs to her room. Once there she flopped down on her bed. "This is getting tiresome," she groused to herself.

"Then do something about it." Salem trotted into the room. "Zelda told you to use your own resources, didn't she?"

"But when it comes to magic, Aunt Zelda and Aunt Hilda *are* my resources."

"You're forgetting one little thing." The cat used his tail to point at a thick leather-bound book sitting on a stand by Sabrina's bed.

Sabrina sat up. "My magic book! Of course!" She snatched the huge volume off the stand and opened it to the index. "What do I look under?"

"Try *pets.*"

"There are pet stores in the Other Realm?"

"How else do you think witches buy supplies for their familiars?"

That sounded logical. To her surprise, Sabrina found several listings for pet stores in the index. "Critter City: Food and Fashion for Your Familiar," she read. "Higher Scales Reptile Supplies . . . Walter Witch's Discount Pet Place . . . ah, this sounds like a good one here—Mr. Ichth's Aqua-World." She flipped to the right page. "Look, Salem, it's even got a direct book portal."

"Then let's hop through it," said Salem.

Sabrina set her Magic Book, open to the page with the ad on it, down on the bed. Salem leaped into her arms and the two of them were sucked into the book itself, right into the picture in the ad.

"Wait, we didn't check the store hours," Sabrina said as she and Salem materialized on a stone walkway that led to Mr. Ichth's Aqua-World. No ground existed on either side of the walkway. The path simply hung in open space, like a ribbon in the sky. Sabrina was used to bizarre phenomenon like this in the Other Realm. Once she'd gotten used to traveling through her aunts' linen closet, everything else was just one more oddity of witch life.

"Hours are no problem," Salem was telling her. "Look."

A flashing neon sign in the window of the store read ALWAYS OPEN. That was one thing about the Other Realm that Sabrina really liked—retail places kept long hours. Witch schedules weren't like mortal schedules, after all. Witches stayed up late into the night, if they ever went to bed at all. Shopping at midnight was commonplace.

"So let's get this over with, shall we?" Salem urged. "All this fish nonsense is making me hungry."

Sabrina set the impatient cat on the walkway, then held the door open for him so he could enter. What happened next took her completely by surprise.

The interior of Mr. Ichth's Aqua-World was, quite literally, underwater. A rippling wall of water lay just beyond the door, and Sabrina and Salem walked right into it before they even registered its existence.

Salem immediately started floating. "I'm wet!" he screeched in a gurgly underwater voice. "I'm a cat, and I'm wet! This is *not* nice!"

Sabrina automatically started treading water. "Drat, my hair will be all messed up, but at least we can breathe."

"Of course you can breathe," came a deep, bubbly voice. "It wouldn't do me any good to kill my customers, now would it?" A halibut the size of a football player swam up to them. "I am Mr. Ichth, owner of this establishment. You may call me Mr. Ichth."

So much for being used to bizarre phenomenon. Sabrina was so startled by the sight of the giant halibut that she jumped, but since she was underwater, the jerky motion didn't really show.

What *did* show was her pained expression as Salem reached out and dug his claws into her arm. It was the only way he could keep from floating away. Sabrina managed to say through gritted teeth, "Nice to meet you, Mr. Ichth."

The halibut flicked his left pectoral fin in greeting. "So what brings you here?" he asked, turning a bit so that his huge bulgy eyes, both of which were located on the same side of his head, could see her. Sabrina had never seen a halibut, but she'd learned in school that as they matured, one eye literally migrated around the head to meet the other, making them look like creatures out of a Picasso painting. The sight of one this big was unsettling, but he seemed very nice and exceptionally polite.

"I have some questions about fish," Sabrina said, trying to ignore his two eyes.

"Just ask your questions and let's get out of here," grumped Salem. "I'm good for maybe two minutes, then *something's* going to get eaten."

Sabrina nodded. Salem's fur floated freely in the gentle current, making him look as if he'd just been through a fluff cycle in the dryer. "I recently moved an aquarium," she said, "and I don't think the fish are happy about it."

Mr. Ichth immediately seemed concerned. The protruding oval of his fish lips quivered as he rhythmically sucked in water, shooting it back out his gills. "What kind of tank is it?"

"What do you mean? It holds water and fish swim around inside."

"I mean, is it freshwater or marine?"

"Oh. Uh . . ." Sabrina thought about it. "Marine."

"Cold water or tropical?"

"Uhh . . ." This took more effort. "Well, the miniature city is designed to look Greek, so I guess that means—"

"Tropical," finished Mr. Ichth. "What species are present?"

"Uhh . . ." Again Sabrina thought hard. "I saw a bunch of what looked like little sharks, and there are some really colorful things, and Salem says one of them's a puffer fish—"

"In other words, you have no idea," cut in Mr. Ichth. "What kind of filtration system do you have?"

Now Sabrina was totally lost. "Filtration system . . . ?"

"Okay, let's cut to the chase," Salem snapped. "She's an aquarium neophyte and I'm a wet cat. Sell her a book or something so we can get out of here."

"It's not that easy," Mr. Ichth bubbled sternly. "Filtration is essential. And what about aeration? Heating? Has the bio-environment been properly established? Have you checked the pH level? What's the reading on your hydrometer? Do you have proper lighting? What do you feed the residents and how often?"

"I don't know any of that!" Sabrina blurted out.

"You'd better find out," bubbled Mr. Ichth,

"or you may find yourself with a tank full of dead fish in a very short time."

Sabrina blanched. "How short a time might that be?"

Mr. Ichth didn't have eyelids, but somehow his round eyes took on a hard glare. "Mere hours."

Sabrina turned to Salem, who was still holding on to her sleeve with his claws. "Salem, we have to get to school right away! I know what's wrong!" She started swimming for the door.

Mr. Ichth darted after her. "Wait! At least take one of these free pamphlets. It's by no means complete, but it lists the basics of aquarium care."

Sabrina took the pamphlet from his proffered fin. "Thanks!"

Once outside on the stone path, she dried herself and Salem by zapping a big blow dryer on them, then the book portal sucked them back to the mortal realm.

Chapter 6

☆

So what's the panic?" Salem asked her as they materialized in Sabrina's room. "What's wrong with the aquarium?"

"You know how Mr. Ichth mentioned a filtration system and all that stuff?" Sabrina asked nervously. "Salem, the aquarium doesn't *have* one!"

Salem nodded. "I'd say that's a big bingo."

One quick zap and they were back at the Mesmer estate. The hallway looked much different now—dark and silent with only the pale moonlight that sifted through a row of stained-glass skylights to see by. The portraits of Augustus Mesmer's ancestors frowned down from inside their heavy mahogany frames, their stern countenances eerie in the shadows, their painted eyes following Sabrina's every move.

Salem trotted along at her side. "Nice place after dark. So where does Dracula keep his coffin?"

"Oh, be quiet," Sabrina snapped, feeling edgy. She wasn't usually the kind to get scared in spooky old houses, but she and Harvey had recently seen the horror film *I'll Be Glad When You're Dead, You Slasher You, Part XIII*. In these midnight hues, Mesmer's hallway resembled the one in the film where a teenage boy had met a grisly fate at the hands of an escaped lunatic with a portable paper shredder.

Sabrina rushed down the hallway to the aquarium suite and examined the floor where the aquarium had stood. Sure enough, there were several holes drilled into the wood, and various tubes disappeared into whatever room lay beneath. The tops of the tubes looked as if they'd been cut off with scissors. "I had no idea a transportation spell could do that," Sabrina said, indicating the tubes.

"Well, if the object you're transporting is attached to other objects, all of them don't automatically move," Salem told her. "Magic only transports the items that you focus on at any given time."

"Great." Hunkering down on her hands and knees, Sabrina tried to see what lay beyond the drilled holes below. "It's too dark to see, but I bet all the filtration equipment is down there. I've got to get it!" She poised her finger.

"Whoa, whoa, whoa!" said Salem. "What do you intend to do?"

"Zap us down there, of course."

"Without knowing what it looks like? What if it's not a whole room, just a crawl space? I may be small, but I'd really rather not materialize inside a shoebox-size space."

Sabrina got to her feet. "Good idea." She considered her options. "How about a beeper spell?"

Salem nodded. "Now you're thinking."

Pleased, Sabrina searched her jacket pocket. "Here—I'll put a spell on this extra button so that it beeps." She dropped it through one of the holes in the floor. She heard it *plink* onto a surface below.

Scooping Salem up in her arms, Sabrina went out into the hallway and down the first flight of stairs she could find. Listening carefully, she heard a faint *beep beep.*

Stumbling a little, Sabrina hurried along in the dark, clutching Salem as she honed in on the beeping. Eventually she was guided to a small door set in a dark alcove, out of the way of the main hallway. "It must be in here," Sabrina told Salem.

"Then open it."

The little door was locked, but Sabrina opened it with an unlocking spell. Salem had been right about one thing—the room was small. Only slightly larger than a closet, it was filled with the last thing Sabrina had expected to find: technology that could only have come from the Other Realm.

Sabrina gasped. "Mesmer was a *witch?*"

Chapter 7

☆

"Look at this stuff!" Sabrina murmured in awe.

The aquarium equipment wasn't modern looking; it was more like a complicated series of gadgets from a Jules Verne novel. The tubes from the aquarium suite above were attached to bizarre fixtures on various elaborate, multi-chambered pumps and filter systems, all made of glistening Other Realm metals. Bubblers bubbled, filters cleaned, charcoal purified, but there was no water to filter now. Mesmer's equipment was running perfectly, except that it wasn't hooked up to anything.

"I feel like we should shut it off, but I have no idea how," Salem said. "It's probably spell driven. But this certainly answers a few questions I had about this place—just think, ol' Mesmer was a witch!"

"All this time, there's been another witch in

Westbridge," said Sabrina, "and we never knew."

"Oh, there could be lots of witches in West-bridge," Salem noted. "Most are smart enough to blend in with the locals."

"Well, this makes one thing clear. I have to find another way to save the fish."

Sabrina zapped Salem and herself back to the Westbridge High maintenance building. "If only I could just solve this whole mess with magic. But if this is going to become part of a permanent learning center, the filter system can't be built of Other Realm materials."

"I have a question," Salem said, gazing into the tank. "Do fish swim upside down?"

Sabrina squealed. "Eek! They're dying!" She didn't need a Looky-Loop to see the few small forms floating belly up, still alive but definitely not long for the world. The rest of the fish gulped at the surface of the water. Dozens of tiny shadows hung limp and motionless around the city as well. "Salem, I have to do something!" Sabrina fluttered her hands around. "What can I do?"

"Save them from a lingering death by letting me eat them?" suggested the cat. "After all, they *do* look like little hors d'oeuvres."

Sabrina ignored him. "Oxygen," she muttered. "I've got to give them oxygen." She pointed at the tank. A large bubble of gas formed above the mountain and rocketed to the surface, bursting through it with a loud pop. Startled fish scattered everywhere, then slowly headed for the surface again, gasping.

"Okay, close but no cigar. I've got to make smaller bubbles. Wait—" An idea struck her. She pointed at the tank with a corkscrew twist of her wrist. An electric mixer appeared over the water, its beaters churning air into the water.

The fish backed away to safety, then slowly began to recover, their movements becoming more energetic. Encouraged, Sabrina repeated her corkscrew gesture until a dozen mixers were blending water and air. In a few minutes all the fish were recovering.

"This can only be a temporary solution, Salem. I need to think of something more permanent . . . and more normal."

"Get the cheerleaders to take turns working the mixers. It'll be the closest they've ever come to working in their lives."

"Ha ha. Now come up with a *helpful* suggestion."

Salem trotted to the back of the aquarium and studied the tubes that hung down from the top— tubes that had been cut off by Sabrina's transportation spell. "Why not do what Mesmer did?" he finally suggested.

"Oh, right," said Sabrina. "Import Frankenstein's laboratory into the middle of Westbridge High. That'll give everyone something to talk about—right before they tattoo *witch* on my forehead and make me wear one of those ugly pointy hats."

"No," said Salem, "hide the equipment in the basement. It worked for Mesmer, didn't it?"

Sabrina thought about it. "He lived alone, Salem. I'd never be able to hide anything for long around here, not with Mr. Kraft snooping around." She sighed. "There's only thing I can do—I have to get some mortal aquarium equipment, fast. But how can I keep the fish alive in the meantime?" A nasty idea came to her mind. "Salem, how would you like to operate some eggbeaters while I'm gone?"

Salem's ears flattened. "How about you just freeze the tank?"

"Freeze it? I can't freeze it! The fish would die!"

"No, no. Use the spell that Zelda puts on Hilda's cooking. You remember—for the stuff that no one wants to eat but is too dangerous to throw in the trash?"

"Oh, you mean like her recipe for Chewy Fudge Bombs?"

"Exactly." Salem shivered at the memory. "The first piece exploded, and it took me a week to get the chocolate out of my fur."

Sabrina didn't have *The Discovery of Magic* with her, nor had she ever seen the complete recipe for Zelda's "stasis spell," but she had seen her aunt conjure up the ingredients once. "Let's see—I'll need a watch, a hammer, and a plastic container."

The items appeared on a table. "Nice watch," commented Salem. "Too bad I don't have wrists."

"You can't have it anyway," said Sabrina, and without another word she snatched up the hammer and brought it down on the watch, *wham!* Then she dumped the munched pieces of ex-watch into the plastic container while chanting,

> *"Time has stopped this moment cold*
> *But will resume when it is told."*

With that, she sealed the plastic container and set it on the aquarium. Instantly a magical effect spread from the plastic container down into the aquarium, stopping everything. "There," said Sabrina happily. "All the little fishies will stay just like this until we get back."

"We?"

"Yes, *we.* You're coming with me."

"Where?"

"Hmm. Good question." Sabrina had forgotten how late it was again. Where was she going to find a mortal pet store open after midnight? "I bet Aunt Hilda would know. She knows just about every retail store on Earth."

"Forget it. She won't help you, remember?"

"Then"—Sabrina racked her brain—"I'll help myself!" Scooping Salem up into her arms, she chanted,

"By Earth and Fire, Sea and Sky,
West or East, I want to fly
To find a store that's open now
To fix my tank, they'll show me how."

Everything around Sabrina and Salem spun like a crazed carousel, and suddenly they were traveling at a furious pace even though they were standing still. An instant later the weird sense of motion slowed enough for Sabrina to make out a green jewel of an island in an ultramarine bay far, far below. "We're in the sky!" she said, but that situation abruptly changed as the island came barreling up at her at what looked like a zillion miles an hour. Or was she falling down to the island? Either way, her stomach did a double flip.

And then she was standing outside a small shop covered with signs that were all written in Chinese characters.

"Pinch my nose for me," Salem said, shaking his head. "After a landing like that, I gotta pop my ears."

"Wow, we're in China!" Sabrina said in awe.

"Looks like Hong Kong," Salem corrected her.

"Cool!" Setting the cat down, Sabrina stepped into the store to find herself at one end of an aisle that looked more like a path through an over-stocked warehouse than an aisle in a retail showroom. Fish tanks and aquariums stacked four and five high formed the walls, each filled with exotic finny forms. Netting hung from the ceiling with brightly printed boxes of fish products tucked inside. Salem couldn't help licking his chops compulsively as he walked past more fish than he'd ever seen in his life.

The labyrinth finally opened into a cramped space in front of a black and red lacquer counter. Beyond the counter a tiny woman in a green silk *cheong-sam* smiled at Sabrina from atop a bamboo stool. Her black hair was streaked with gray and tied into a tight bun at the back of her head.

Sabrina racked her brain to remember a spell so that when English was spoken, the shop owner would hear only Chinese, and when the shop keeper replied in Chinese it would be translated into English automatically.

Sabrina had to try two spells to find one that would do. "I hope you can help me. I have a large tank that I had to move from one place to another, and it needs . . . well, whatever it is that keeps the fish from dying." It seemed to be working as the older woman nodded, obviously understanding.

"I see," she answered. "And is there a reason why you cannot use the equipment from the original tank setting?"

"Well, you see, it's sort of . . . customized. The stuff it used before doesn't, uh . . . match the new decor."

"How exactly was the equipment customized?"

"It's just really . . . foreign. For one thing, it doesn't use electricity." Sabrina waved her hands helplessly. "Let's just say it's unique."

The little Chinese woman nodded again, her dark eyes flashing with understanding as if the mysteries of all the universe were clear now. "I see. I take it the equipment is witch powered."

"Exactly. I mean, *no!* I mean . . ." Sabrina gave a casual laugh that rang false even to her own ears. "What made you say something as silly as that? Heh heh."

The woman gestured. "Because your cat is speaking to himself."

Sure enough, Salem had his face and paws pressed against the glass of a koi tank and was crooning to the big colorful fish inside. "Oohh, you look so yummy! Swim this way, you seven course meal you!" Several of the giant goldfish floated eye to eye with Salem, their mouths puckering open and closed as if they considered the cat a tasty snack and were trying to find a way to nibble him through the glass.

"Salem, stop that!" Sabrina snapped.

"Stop what?" Salem put a paw over his mouth. "I mean—oops!"

"Do not be alarmed," said the Chinese woman. "I could tell right away that you were both witches."

Salem was intrigued. "How? The glow of vast intellect shining in my eyes?"

"No, the fact that I saw you speaking to each

other before you entered my store." She gestured over her head. "Witchcraft can tell you much, but nothing beats a good surveillance camera." She stepped out from behind the counter, revealing the full length of her beautiful green silk dress and her dainty slippers. "I take it your aquarium must be displayed in public, so you may no longer use its original setup."

"Something like that," Salem drawled.

"Describe it." The woman sat down on a stool beside a rickety wooden table, her hands poised as if she were about to sculpt clay, except that there was nothing on the table.

"Well, it's really big and square, maybe"—Sabrina looked around—"as long as those three tanks over there combined. It sits on a special pedestal."

The woman moved her hands gracefully in the air, and a model of a square fish tank on a pedestal appeared on the table. It wasn't a real one but was carved from ivory, and the pedestal looked like solid jade. Sabrina nearly gasped— as a piece of artwork, it was beautiful. "Does the tank stand against a wall?" the woman asked.

"No, students are going to be able to walk all the way around it," Sabrina answered, then she paused. "Can I ask what exactly you're doing?"

The woman continued to move her hands over the ivory miniature, saying as she did, "I am casting what is called a Parallela-Spell. The miniature tank before your eyes represents the real one. I will create miniatures of the equipment you need, and as it forms on this model tank, so it will form on your tank in its appropriate size." She grinned. "It is so much easier than selling you equipment you will not know how to set up."

"Good call," Salem agreed.

For the next few minutes the Chinese witch waved her hands over the miniature tank, announcing each piece of equipment as she created it and telling Sabrina how it worked and what maintenance it required. When she was finished, the ivory tank shimmered brightly, then disappeared. "It is done. You may return home."

"What about payment?" asked Sabrina. "All I have is American money." She dug into her pocket and frowned. "And not much of that."

The woman gazed at her. "Where do you live?"

"Westbridge."

"Then consider this a favor. If I ever visit Westbridge, I will expect a tour. Acceptable?"

"Very!" Sabrina thanked the woman, scooped up Salem, and zapped them both to Westbridge High's maintenance building. "Perfect!" she said, examining the augmented aquarium. Pumps, filters, and bubblers were pumping, filtering, and bubbling away.

"Nothing's happening," Salem noted.

"Oops! Forgot." Sabrina snatched the plastic container off the aquarium and opened it up. Pouring the broken watch fragments into one hand, she intoned,

*"Broken watch, be whole and run
To make this stasis spell be done."*

The watch reassembled itself, and the fish in the tank snapped back to life. "There! Now I think"—she suddenly yawned—"it's time for bed. I'm pooped."

"No go. Look at the watch," said Salem.

Sabrina looked at the clicking watch in her hands. "Seven forty-five? Omigosh, it's time for school!"

Chapter 8

☆

☆

Sabrina slogged her way down the hall to her locker, struggling to keep her backpack on her slumping shoulders. Ever since she realized the time, she had been yawning. *I haven't pulled an all-nighter like this in months. Lucky Salem,* she thought ruefully. *He can just curl up and go to sleep now. And knowing cats, he'll still be asleep when I get home.*

"Sabrina!" The voice belonged to Valeric, who hurried up to Sabrina with an expression of worry. "Mr. Kraft is looking for you. He's been going up and down the halls asking everybody where you are."

Sabrina yawned. "That's nice."

"Nice? He's the VP! So what's the story? Are you in some kind of trouble?"

Before Sabrina could answer, the call of "Miss Spellman!" carried down the hall.

At the sound of Kraft's voice, Valerie cringed. "Good luck. Gotta go." She darted away as Mr. Kraft approached, brandishing an aerosol can and spraying it before him as if clearing a path through an odorous jungle. Students shied away from him, sneezing and holding their noses and mumbling complaints.

"Heard that!" Kraft barked at one boy who had muttered too loudly. The VP paused to scribble the boy's name on his ever-present detention pad. As he did, Sabrina's foggy brain registered what was going on.

Mr. Kraft? she wondered. Then, "Yikes—Mr. Kraft!"

He stopped before her. "Yikes, Miss Spellman? Is that some kind of new greeting?" With that, he sprayed the air between them.

It made Sabrina sneeze.

"So I was right!" Kraft said triumphantly. "There *is* some kind of epidemic going around. First Gordie, then Desmond, now you. What are the other symptoms? Congestion? Headache? Muscle pain? What are you doing here, anyway? Don't you have enough sense not to come to school when you're sick?"

Sabrina waved her hand in front of her face, trying to dissipate whatever Kraft had loosened in the air. "It's that spray," she said, indicating the aerosol can.

"This is disinfectant," Kraft told her sternly. "I can't afford to get sick, not now. And speaking of now, I'd like you to take a little trip with me."

Sabrina stifled a yawn. "This minute?"

"That's usually what *now* means." He stared hard at her face. "You look terrible. I just hope for your sake you're not contagious."

"Really, Mr. Kraft, I'm not sick—"

"Yes, you are." He sprayed the air again, and Sabrina sneezed again. "Just come with me— but keep your distance."

As Sabrina suspected, Mr. Kraft led her to the school maintenance building. Standing before the aquarium, he heaved a loud sigh. "What is the meaning of this?"

"Meaning?" Sabrina asked innocently. "You told me to move the aquarium. So I moved the aquarium."

"Yes, but *how?*" demanded Kraft. "It hasn't been twenty-four hours since you first saw it. And you were supposed to order plastic containers from me, remember?"

Sabrina thought fast. "Yes, well . . . that would have been an excellent way to get the job done, Mr. Kraft, and I was certainly planning on it, but, uh, the very first phone call I made yesterday was to an aquarium mover who, uh, wanted to contribute to the local community so he moved it all for free." That sounded good. She smiled hopefully at him.

Mr. Kraft didn't smile back. "You make me doubt your truthfulness, Miss Spellman. No reputable business does *anything* for free. It would be a terrible precedent to set."

"He was a really nice guy . . . with a new

business." She shrugged. "I guess he did it for the good will."

Mr. Kraft didn't move a muscle, and Sabrina was tempted to flick her finger just enough to cast a mind-reading spell. *Is he mad at me?* she wondered. *Or is he impressed?* She couldn't tell.

That was when Kraft stuffed the aerosol can into his jacket pocket with a little grunt of defeat. "Under the circumstances, I suppose I ought to congratulate you then."

Sabrina relaxed. "Thanks."

"Mind you, I'm extremely curious as to how you *really* got this tank here, but somehow I know"—and he stared hard at her—"that I'll never learn the truth. Not from you, anyway. Therefore, I'll accept your explanation." Sabrina tensed again, but to her relief, Kraft let the subject go. Instead he said, "The only problem is that your hyper-efficiency prevented you from hearing of my plans for this particular item."

"Plans?"

"Yes. You see, I don't want the fish. Or the Greek city. In fact, I was planning on having you remove all the contents from the tank except the gravel and some of the plants."

Now Sabrina was really confused. "Why do you want Mesmer's fish tank if there are no fish in it?"

"Because this tank," Kraft explained, "is going to be used for a more educational purpose. In this very space I am going to conduct miniature reenactments of the world's historic sea battles, beginning with the great battle in 1805 when British Admiral Viscount Horatio Nelson defeated the French and Spanish fleets at Cape Trafalgar." Instantly caught up in his grand vision of naval history, he started circling the tank. "Every month a new scenario. I'll reenact the Boston Tea Party—the mystery of the *Andrea Doria*—the sinking of the *Titanic!*"

"But what about Mesmer's legacy?"

"Ah, there's the beauty of it," Kraft told her. "This tank will actually *generate* revenue for the school! What better legacy could there be? For a modest fee, I'll invite the public to the school to watch the reenactments—a sort of adult education program. And the school film club can tape each performance for use as a visual aid in future history classes. I can even rent copies out to other schools! The possibilities are endless! And of course, all fish and equipment will be sold off to fund the reenactments." He rubbed his hands in anticipation. "Being an entrepreneur himself, I'm sure Mesmer would understand."

Even Sabrina could understand such a plan, strange as it was. At least there was some educational value to it. But if the aquarium had belonged to Mesmer, and Mesmer was a witch, there was no telling what could happen. For all she knew, the fish were Other Realm species, unique, maybe priceless. Perhaps they needed this exact environment to survive. Moving them within their own environment was one thing— removing them from it was another.

"But this isn't an ordinary aquarium, Mr. Kraft," she said. "I mean, I think these fish might be rare species. Shouldn't we find out—?"

"No time," interrupted Kraft. "I want the Trafalgar scenario ready for next Monday. That's when the district school board meets next, and it just so happens that they're meeting here." Kraft stepped over to the corner of the maintenance room and snatched up a stepladder. "Bring me that bucket," he instructed her, pointing.

Wondering what he was going to do, Sabrina obeyed. Kraft set the stepladder next to the aquarium, climbed up, opened a section of the aquarium lid, and after pulling back his sleeve, plunged his hand into the water. Fish scattered as he reached around, grabbing at plants. Snaring several of them in his fingers, he pulled them up, loosening great billows of sand and muck from the mini-ocean floor, making the tank look as if a miniature bomb had exploded.

"What are you doing?" Sabrina squealed.

"No time like the present," Kraft answered as he handed a fistful of the dripping plants to her. "There, I've started the job for you. Now I want you to finish it before you go home." At Sabrina's look of dismay, he added, "That's right, you're going home. You're sick. I'll get enough plastic containers for the fish later." He descended the stepladder and flicked water from his fingers. "And get that model village out of there. What an eyesore." With that, he left.

Sabrina stood there alone, shocked, exhausted, and with a pile of dripping sea plants in her hands. In dismay she looked down at the greenery, only to receive another shock—snagged in the plants were several tiny, green, gasping human figures, only these figures had long fish tails instead of legs. Sabrina's eyes nearly popped out of her head.

There were *mermaids* in the fish tank!

Chapter 9

$\bigstar$

$\bigstar$

Sabrina gawked at the tiny green people in her hands. They gawked back at her, their little eyes wide, both in shock and from the effects of slow asphyxiation. "Omigosh, I'm sorry!" Sabrina suddenly blurted out, and she tossed the plants back into the aquarium. With so much debris stirred up, it was hard for her to tell where the mermaids were now, but she presumed they were recovering.

"I've got to get to the bottom of this," she told herself firmly, "which means"—she contemplated the aquarium—"I've got to get to the bottom of *that!*"

She didn't know how to scuba dive. In fact, she wasn't all that good a swimmer. But thanks to witch magic, Sabrina came up with a perfect plan. Concentrating, she pointed her finger at herself.

Everything flashed white.

The next thing Sabrina knew, she was floating weightlessly in an empty space. Sounds were muffled, as if her ears were plugged, and just beyond her outstretched fingertips, water hung suspended, forced away by an invisible wall.

She was inside a tiny bubble of air.

Like a blimp descending for a landing, Sabrina's bubble floated gently down through the aquarium water, down, down toward the village on the underwater hill. Passing fish eyed her curiously, and one even tried to bite her bubble, but to Sabrina's relief, it couldn't get a firm hold and only bumped her off course a bit.

At this tiny size Sabrina could make out the details on the community of beautiful villas and buildings clustered around an enormous palace complex that crowned the aquarium's mini-mountain.

A green blur flashed by. Then another. Looking up, Sabrina saw the merpeople she had freed from the uprooted plants. Most were still milling about in confusion, but several were heading back home, flashing by her at great speed as if in some kind of hurry. *Duh,* she thought. *They probably just had the scare of their lives.*

Then another flash of color caught her attention. From below came a murky gleam of gold, then another. A squad of armored mermen, each carrying a wickedly pointed trident, was swimming up to meet her. The squad split up as they neared, making a ring around her bubble and dropping their weapons to the ready position.

The leader of the squad, a husky merman with dark-green hair and a bite-shaped piece of his fluke missing, brought the points of his trident to the edge of Sabrina's balloon and spoke. To her surprise, she heard him clearly, despite the water separating them. "Set the bubble down in the courtyard, kid," he ordered in a flat, no-nonsense tone. "Move slow and nothing will get punctured." He raised his other hand, in which he held a fist-size conch shell as if it were a radio handset. "Tell the Hereditary Maav-En that we've got another sign of the End Times here," he barked into it.

He moved the conch away from his mouth, and a tiny shrimplike creature darted out of the shell, swimming briskly toward the palace. The merman ignored it, instead concentrating his attention on the strange visitor.

All Sabrina could think to do was wave. "So, you guys root for the Dolphins down here?"

He continued to stare.

"Silly me, I should have known. You probably can't get cable underwater, right?"

Still nothing but the stare.

"Look, I didn't mean to cause any problems. I just didn't know you were here. Can we pretend it never happened and start over from the beginning? I'll go first, if that helps." She held out her hand to shake, then realized it was a stupid gesture. Not only might mermaids not shake hands upon greeting, but she couldn't touch anything outside her bubble anyway. "I'm Sabrina. What's your name?"

The guard's attitude changed immediately. "It's about time you bothered to ask," he said with a haughty sniff. "I'm Amun Rahrah, Major Domo of the Life Guards, Captain of Palace Security and Ad-Hoc Chairman of the Seaweed Abatement Task Force."

"Wow, a Type-A personality, eh?"

"It's a job." Amun-Rahrah preened. "Besides, *somebody* has to see that things get done around here. Not that doing a good job gets appreciated, noooo. Well, it doesn't matter. It's the end of the world for us, but at least we'll go knowing that the head bureaucrats are going, too."

It was Sabrina's turn to stare.

"Ah, pay no attention to that flounder-headed radical," a quavering voice broke in. While the guard had been declaiming, a trio of ancient-looking merfolk had glided out of the castle. Two of them were old males, balding and afflicted with occasional shudders. Deep bags puddled beneath their watery eyes. Both wore heavily embroidered ceremonial vests. The older male's vest had more gold trim, but the younger one's vest had more medals and a pouch filled with scrolls. The merwoman who swam along with the males had a kelp-forest of faded green hair trailing in the water behind her, and she wore a shawl that looked as if it was crocheted from anemones.

"Pay no attention, I say," repeated the eldest merman to Sabrina. "He doesn't know what he's talking about." He turned a baleful eye on Amun Rahrah and snapped, "And *someone's* going to drop like a rock if he doesn't remember his job and make proper introductions. It's not like the Keftiu government meets with the Visitation of Doom every weekend."

Amun Rahrah threw back his shoulders and, bowing to Sabrina, proclaimed, "Keftiu welcomes you, O Conch Queen, Bringer of Doom! As it was written, 'We were expecting this any day now.' Greeting you on behalf of our people and our city, I present Ugawp, Hereditary Maav-En and Sitter on the Clamshell Throne.

"Assisting in managing the burdens of state is—" Amun Rahrah continued in his proclamation voice.

"Not so fast, kiddo," interrupted the merwoman. "Since when does the chief's wife get upstaged?"

The slightly less-ancient merman named Phinikas hissed at her, "This is a formal occasion. I'm next. That's protocol."

"You know what you can do with your protocol, Phinikas," the old merwoman snorted. "By protocol I should get introduced next."

Ugawp waved a gnarly hand at Phinikas. "Go ahead, let him introduce her next."

Amun Rahrah cleared his throat again, booming out, "Presenting the Counterweight of State,

the Loyal Opposition and Honored Wife of the
Hereditary Maav-En, Hyppshot."

"Pleased to meet you," Hyppshot said to
Sabrina. She jerked her thumb at her husband.
"Don't make too much of Lord Blowfish, here.
He still puts his vest on one arm at a time, just
like the rest of us."

Amun Rahrah ignored her speech and contin-
ued. "Assisting in managing the burdens of
State— I present Phinikas, holder of the office of
Kronii-Balonii, Grand Vizier to the Throne."
Amun Rahrah gestured toward Sabrina. "Good
worthies of Keftiu, I present the great Conch
Queen, she who is the Visitation of Doom, as
foretold and forewritten."

Sabrina had no idea what was happening, so
she just smiled as charmingly as she could.
"Glad to meet you—I think. But let me make
one teensy correction here—I'm not the Conch
Queen of Doom or whatever."

"We'll be the judge of that, dearie," Hyppshot
said.

Sabrina opened her mouth to reply when
Ugawp inquired of Phinikas, "Has she fulfilled
the Signs?"

Phinikas fished a scroll out of his vest pouch,
unrolled it, and pressed his nose against it,
squinting to read the fine print. "Ahum . . . vast
disruptions, difficulty breathing, citizen abduc-
tions to hostile environs, mass sightings of Giant
Faces . . ." The old merman peered at Sabrina

over the top of the scroll. "Except for there being no mention of the Visitation being female, I'd say she's it."

"Then we are at the End of All. This is a fortunate day!" Ugawp raised his hands and twitched magnificently.

A crowd of merpeople had gathered, and they cheered Ugawp's drastic pronouncement with wild applause and a few bubbly whistles of approval.

Sabrina couldn't remember having been this confused since her aunt Hilda had taken up horseback riding in the living room. It was an activity that hadn't lasted long. "Uh, guys," she said meekly, "even if I were the Conch Queen of Doom—which I'm not—why would you be glad that everything's going to end? Don't you kind of have this backward?"

Ugawp broke off his twitching and stared at Sabrina in surprise. "Not at all. This means that all the stern warnings of our ancestors were right. For generations parents have warned children that lax lives will lead to Doom, just as it did centuries ago. Well, you're the proof!"

Sabrina wasn't sure how to take that, but she had no time to comment. Hyppshot floated close to her bubble and said, "My esteemed husband is wrong most of the time, but for this once I agree with him." She spread her arms to indicate the entire mountaintop city. "Once our people lived on dry land—okay, you could call it a desert, and we did, with lots of moaning and complaining. So what happens? We get turned into merfolk and dumped in the sea. We had it bad and things got worse." She shook her head in despair.

"We complained to the neighbors about how unfair it all was. And what did those stuck-up Egyptians do?" Ugawp took up the tale with some heat, as if the insults had been directed at him personally. "Did they help us? Did they thank us for pointing out the unfairness of life? Did they at least give us a good write-up in their myths? No! They had the nerve to complain about us swimming up to their docks and ships to gripe!"

Amun Rahrah concluded the grand tale. "Our ancestors were tough. They convened the leaders and the greatest magicians of the Keftiu and complained to the Other Realm, who swore to solve our problems but who did no such thing. They only wanted to shut us up. They never consulted the ordinary Keftiuns, and so of course, they only made things worse."

Phinikas had fumbled out three more scrolls and was juggling them from hand to hand, comparing versions and waiting to speak again. He held up a green scroll. "There are two competing schools of thought on what happened next. The Doomsayers believe that things only get worse and that therefore the disappearance of all other life in the world was an inevitable progression of our misery." He tucked that scroll under his arm and waved a different scroll—pale blue, this time. "The Catastrophists, on the other hand, believe that the Universe just has it in for the Keftiu people. They hold that Bad Things are always Just Around the Corner and that they're timed to make us miserable."

Hyppshot turned on him like a shark. "You think that the Visitation of Doom doesn't know this already? She wouldn't be here if Doom wasn't at hand! Anyway, you never answered her question, which is obviously a test."

"No, really, it—" Sabrina began, but Ugawp swam close to her.

"We eagerly await the coming of Doom because it will settle once and for all who has properly interpreted the lessons that were written for us by our ancestors," he whispered conspiratorially. "With one gesture of your mighty hand, O Doom, generations of debate, not to mention several fortunes in side bets, will be settled for all time."

"Yeah, but—" Sabrina said.

"We're good sports about being destroyed as long as we know our enemies are suffering, too," interrupted Amun Rahrah. "Very democratic, in that respect, at least."

"I see that, but—"

"What sport?" shouted Hyppshot to Amun Rahrah. "It's triumph, pure and simple! We Doomsayers may be about to perish, but we will know that those clam-headed Catastrophists follow us—knowing that they are dead wrong!"

Sabrina spoke louder. "Look, please—"

"Never!" roared Phinikas. He shook his pouch of scrolls at the leader's wife, jarring several scrolls loose to drift in the water. "Nowhere is it written that the Catastrophists are wrong! Hundreds of commentaries on the Tragic History of the Keftiu support our view. When the False Great Giant Heads are chased away by the True Great Giant Head, he'll laugh at us like he did at our ancestors, proving that he's had it in for us throughout Eternity!"

"All right, *enough already!*"

The merpeople fell silent and turned to Sabrina as if she were an unruly child who had no right to interfere. Sabrina was just as surprised by her own outburst, but now that she had their attention, she quickly continued, "Okay, here's the deal. I don't know much about *what was written,* but your *whole* world is going to be a write-off if Mr. Kraft has his way. He wants this tank emptied of everything so he can play games. You've got to work with me if you want to survive!"

The merfolk gave Sabrina perfectly blank stares. Then they all began speaking at once, interrupting each other.

"Impossible! First, there is nothing beyond the Hard Water that separates us from the Great Giant Heads. The rest of the world was destroyed centuries ago as documented by—"

"What is this *Kraft* she's talking about? I don't

remember anything by that name mentioned in any writings—"

"You don't remember to put in your false teeth half the time, why should you remember what's written—?"

"Why don't both of you resign and let the working fins take care of themselves as long as Doom is right around the corner? We deserve a taste of freedom before the end—"

"You know, it's not written anywhere that the Visitation of Doom would have legs instead of a fishtail like the rest of us. Maybe she's not the hundred-percent Visitation of Doom, after all. Of course, it'll take me a while to check the scrolls—"

"The question before us becomes, do we prepare for the approaching Doom, even though she's obviously not one of the accredited Signs of the End, or do we consider her as a Sign of the End precisely *because* she's obviously not accredited—?"

The pitch of the arguments rose until Sabrina felt like pulling her hair out. She wanted to help save the merfolk, but their bickering almost made her wish that their Doomsday would arrive.

A loud buzzing sounded inside her air bubble. It was the alarm setting on her watch telling her it was nearly time for class. "I've got to go!" she shouted, trying to be heard over the din of argument.

The Keftiu ignored her.

"Right. Fine. I'll just go then." Sabrina zapped herself out of the aquarium, her mind in a tizzy over how to save a bunch of silly beings who refused to believe they needed saving.

☆

Chapter 10

☆

Sabrina fretted all through English class. What were merpeople doing in Mesmer's aquarium? Were they exotic pets? Were they prisoners? That might explain why they were such a cranky bunch, but even so, why were they so ignorant? Clearly they didn't even know they were in a fish tank.

And why had Mesmer disappeared without leaving any way for the Keftiu to take care of themselves? Sabrina had learned the hard way that witches were capricious, but given their supernatural powers, they were usually pretty responsible types.

But apparently, not in this case. For the last seven years the poor Keftiu had been like sitting ducks, safe only as long as the fish were fed, the tank was cleaned, and no mortals bothered to notice they were in there. Now Kraft was threatening their world, and he was using Sabrina to do it! *Well, I* won't *do it,* she thought. *Maybe I can't stop Mr. Kraft, but I can at least save the Keftiu.*

She skipped lunch and hurried to the maintenance building, which was empty. Until all the Mesmer displays were in place there, nobody was using the space.

Sabrina's plan was simple—she'd remove the Keftiun city, just as Kraft wanted. Thanks to magic, she would easily lift it out of the tank and put it into a carry bucket. Then she'd transport herself home, zap up a temporary tank in her bedroom, and there the Keftiu would stay until after school. Zelda and Hilda would be sure to help once they understood the situation.

Sabrina stood by the aquarium and pointed her finger.

Nothing happened.

She tried again, and this time a bright spark flashed around the base of the city and right into the tip of her pointed finger. Sabrina yelped as a surge of magical power whipped through her like a physical slap.

"It's held down by magic," she muttered in surprise. She'd seen the phenomenon once before when Hilda had tried to snitch a box of chocolates that belonged to Zelda. Zelda had magically affixed the box to the countertop, and when Hilda tried to use magic to float it up to her bedroom, all she'd gotten for her troubles was a backlash of power and a sore finger.

For the next five minutes Sabrina tried valiantly to remove the city, using every magical variation she could imagine. Each attempt created a backlash of power until her finger felt as if it were going to fall off.

Frustrated, she even tried to haul the city out manually, but it wouldn't move. Mesmer obviously intended for the Keftiu to remain put.

Which meant that Kraft couldn't be allowed to keep the tank. *But how can I convince him of that?* Sabrina wondered.

She hurried for the door, glancing at her watch. She had only ten minutes of lunch period left. That might be just enough time, if Kraft was in his office.

He was there, all right, looking like a mad surgeon operating on . . . mail? "Uh, Mr. Kraft?" Sabrina said, gently knocking on his partially open door.

Kraft stood behind his desk, encased in rubber gloves up to his elbows. A pile of mail was heaped on his desk, but it looked damp. He was struggling to open a letter without tearing it to mush when he noticed Sabrina. "Miss Spellman, I'm a busy man. Make it snappy."

"Mr. Kraft," Sabrina said, "the Mesmer aquarium, uhh . . . has a crack in it. You'll have to get another one."

"What?" Kraft slapped down the wet envelope. "Are you sure?"

"Positive. It's only a matter of time till it

cracks more and shatters. You can't keep water in it."

Kraft glared at her. "It was fine when I saw it at Mesmer's estate. That free aquarium mover of yours must have damaged it. I'll sue!"

"No, wait!" Sabrina took a step forward, but Kraft curtly waved a hand, stopping her.

"Stay back," he warned. "If you're contagious, I want you at a distance. In fact, didn't I tell you to go home?"

"Did you?" she asked innocently, realizing that it was her fault that Kraft was so mired in his epidemic fears. After all, if she hadn't made Desmond break out in spots, Kraft probably wouldn't be quite so adamant.

His eyes narrowed. "Yes, I believe I did, Miss Spellman. Now please, do as I say. Whatever you've got will only get worse, and then I'll get it. As it is, I'm having my secretary disinfect all the mail." He picked up the soggy envelope again. "As for the aquarium," he announced, "fix it. That tank was free and so is everything else the school is getting from Mesmer's collection. I'm not going to pay money for another tank when we've got a perfectly good free one that just needs a little repair. If you can't get the job done by Monday, I'll tell Libby to appoint someone who can."

"No!" Sabrina blurted. "No, that won't be necessary. I'll do it. No problem." She backed out of the office. "I can handle it, even if I'm sick."

As she shut the door, Sabrina caught a glimpse of Kraft's secretary handing him another bucket. "Here's the afternoon mail, sir," she said.

Kraft glowered at it.

When Sabrina got home, Zelda and Hilda weren't there. In fact, they didn't show up until after dinnertime, and when they did, they were both in rotten moods.

"———!" Sabrina said excitedly as they stalked into the kitchen.

"Don't bother even trying to talk to us, Sabrina," Hilda said grumpily. "We can't hear you."

"———!" said Sabrina, trying to tell them that she wasn't asking a question about magic. She was trying to tell them about the Keftiu.

"I'm afraid it doesn't matter what subject you pick, dear," Zelda told her.

Hilda smirked. "That's because your aunt, my sister, the brilliant *almost*-Nobel-Prize-winner, dropped a syllable or two when she activated the Oil of Oblivion spell."

"It was a harmless mistake. I misstated the radius variable in the intensity phase of the conjuration. Its effect keeps spreading."

"Try explaining that to the conductor of the Fukuoka Symphony," Hilda snapped, then turned to Sabrina. "I just lost first chair violin because the conductor couldn't hear my playing! I'm so embarrassed. I must have looked like a bad mime."

"———?" Sabrina asked.

"Save it for tomorrow, when the spell wears off." With an angry flourish, Hilda raised her pointing finger. "But I advise someone I know whose name begins with a Z to stay out of my way." And with that, she twirled her finger and a sudden wind scooped her up blew her out the door.

"Uh-oh, she's gone off in a huff," said Zelda. "I'd better go calm her down. The last time she did this, she blew herself all the way to Australia." A twirl of her finger and Zelda sailed out the door as well.

Now that she was alone again, Sabrina's voice returned. "You can stay with the kangaroos if you're not going to help me!" She stamped her foot in frustration. "Grrr, what's the use of yelling if there's nobody around to hear?" As if in reply, the phone rang. Sabrina snatched it up and yelled, "Why won't anybody help me?" into the receiver.

"Sabrina?" came Valerie's hesitant voice. "Did I get the right number? For a second there you sounded enough like me to make me think I'd called myself."

Sabrina calmed down. "Sorry about that," she apologized. "It's just that this stupid Mesmer job's got me crazy. But I'm sure your job is bugging you, too. Oops. Didn't mean to make a bug joke at your expense."

"Actually," Valerie said, "my job's not half bad."

"Really? I thought you hated bugs. Too many legs, you said."

"That's what I thought until I got to know them. Bugs only have six legs. I can handle six. It's spiders that have eight legs. Eight is just too many." She somehow managed to convey a shudder over the phone.

"Well, I'm glad you're doing okay," said Sabrina. "I'm certainly not."

"Can I help?"

Sabrina smiled. Good ol' Valerie. She walked under a self-imposed cloud of doom, but even with that burden, she was always willing to help a friend. "I don't know if you can," said Sabrina, "but at least you can hear me when I talk."

"Sabrina, that is so sweet! That's exactly the way I think about you."

Not sure how she was supposed to take that, Sabrina just said, "Meet me at the Slicery in twenty minutes?"

"Okay, see you there."

Chapter 11

☆

☆

The Slicery walls vibrated with loud music and raucous teenage voices, so Sabrina had to lean in a little to hear what Valerie was saying. "And there are some giant tropical bugs in the collection that are as big as my hand. I keep imagining . . ."

Sabrina took another bite of her pizza and tried to focus on what Val was saying, but she couldn't follow her friend's babbling.

"I'm glad you and the bug world are getting along so well," Sabrina said. "Can we talk about my problem now?"

Valerie gave a guilty start. "Oh. Sorry. Me and my motor mouth. I guess we did come here to talk about you. So what's the problem?"

"My problem is Mr. Kraft."

"Everybody's problem is Mr. Kraft."

Sabrina had to laugh. "No, I mean him and

the Mesmer aquarium. He wants me to dump all the fish and peop—I mean, plants from the tank so he can use it as a playpond for re-creating naval battles."

"Did you know that skimmer bugs can walk on water?" Valerie cut in. "They just glide along like . . . Oh, I did it again. Sorry. Go on."

"Well, I think a lot of the stuff in that aquarium is unique. I think that throwing it all away would be a terrible mistake."

Valerie shrugged. "If Mr. Kraft wants you to get rid of it, what else can you do?"

Sabrina felt the need to lower her voice. That, of course, necessitated that she lean in even closer to Valerie, who automatically leaned closer to her. "I've got to find out more about Mesmer," Sabrina declared. "What if he's actually still alive? Maybe I could find some way to let him know that the Keftiu are doomed unless he comes back."

Valerie gave her a funny look. "The Kefti-*what?*"

"Uh . . . it's a rare species of sea life that can only live in that tank. Anyway, you know journalism stuff. How does somebody go about finding a missing person?"

Valerie took a long sip of her soda. "What about hiring a detective?"

"What about paying him?"

"Oh, right. Well, what about doing what they do in detective shows? I read somewhere that Hollywood writers consult real detectives for procedure. Or how about putting an ad in the paper? Mesmer might see it."

"You've seen those infomercials," Sabrina said. "There are thousands of newspapers across the country. I could place tiny classified ads in them all, but I'd go broke doing it."

Valerie pursed her lips. "Sabrina, I'm trying to help, but you're shooting down every suggestion I make!"

"I'm sorry, it's just that . . . oh, it's probably a stupid idea to look for Mesmer anyway. If he's been gone this long, he's not coming back."

Valerie grew thoughtful. "There's one place you could easily look."

"Where?"

"The morgue."

"Eww!"

"I mean the newspaper morgue—where they keep the clippings of old stories."

"Oh. I knew that." It was a good idea, but Sabrina figured that Mesmer, being a witch, would have been good at avoiding the limelight. Under normal circumstances checking the "morgue" might prove helpful, but she doubted it would turn up anything in this case. "Any other ideas? I have a feeling that Mesmer kept to himself a lot."

Valerie's eyes glazed over as she thought hard, chewing absently on her soda straw. "The only other thing I can think of is that somebody might have filed a missing-persons report on him."

A bell-like *ding-ding-ding!* went off in Sabrina's head. "A missing-persons report! That's it! Valerie, you're great! You've really helped me out!"

"I have?" Valerie broke out in a pleased grin. "Could you tell my mom?"

"As soon as I track this down." Sabrina hopped to her feet and started for the door. "I gotta go!"

"Wait, don't you want to stay to finish the pizza?"

As she hurried out, Sabrina called over her shoulder, "Nah, talking about bugs killed my appetite. Bye, and thanks!"

"Salem! Does the Other Realm have a Missing-Persons Department?"

Sabrina had returned home to find her aunts watching *Fluffy, the Good Little Vampire* on TV. The Oil of Oblivion spell was worse than ever— not only did Zelda and Hilda not hear her speak, but they didn't even hear her enter the house. Knowing it was hopeless to try to get their attention, Sabrina had turned to Salem.

The cat's tail flicked back and forth in little annoyed jerks. "I'll have you know I was asleep, dreaming that I was the well-fed mascot aboard a tuna trawler."

"Sorry about that," said Sabrina, "but this is more important. So?"

"So what?"

"So does the Other Realm have a Missing-Persons Department?"

"I would presume so." Salem yawned. "It's probably part of Lost and Found."

"Then you've got to help me—"

"Aw, not again."

"Yes, again. Salem, Mesmer's fish tank doesn't just contain fish. It contains mermaids!"

The black cat didn't bat an eye. "Really? No wonder his setup is complicated. Mermaids are very finicky about their habitats."

"Y-you . . ." It took a moment for Sabrina to be able to form the words. "You've seen mermaids before?"

"Sure," Salem said. "There are lots of them in the Other Realm. I've never heard of little ones in a fishtank before, though. I guess they can miniaturize anything these days."

"They call themselves the Keftiu," Sabrina explained, "and Mr. Kraft wants me to get rid of them. I mean, he doesn't actually know they're in there, but he wants them gone, and the only thing I can think to do is find Mesmer and tell him." She snatched up *The Discovery of Magic* and checked the index. "Here it is—the Lost and Found Department. C'mon!"

"Hey, wait, I'm not—"

Sabrina picked him up. "Yes, you are. C'mon."

Unlike Mr. Ichth's store, the L&F didn't have a direct book portal, so Sabrina carried Salem into the linen closet. A flash of lightning and a rumble of thunder later, they stood in a quaint little office before an ancient old man who looked as if he'd worn the same business suit for the last hundred years. A dusty nameplate on his battered wooden desk read I. M. CHRONIS, L&F ADMINISTRATOR. He looked more like someone's beloved old grandfather in a TV sitcom.

"No skunks allowed," Chronis greeted Sabrina as she set Salem on the desk.

"I'm not a skunk," Salem snapped. "I'm a cat."

The old man adjusted his glasses and peered at Salem. "No cats allowed."

"He's not really a cat, either," said Sabrina. "He's a witch. He just looks like a cat."

The old man peered over his glasses, then under them. "Looks like a badger."

Salem drew in a breath, no doubt preparing to say something sarcastic. Sabrina silenced him with a glance. "Mr. Chronis, we need to find someone who's missing," she said.

The old man nodded and turned to the computer on his desk. "Name?"

"His or mine?"

Mr. Chronis typed one slow letter at a time. "H-I-S . . . O-R . . ."

"No, no," Salem said, "she asked if you wanted his name or her name."

"What?" Chronis blinked. "The missing person's name, of course. No good giving me your name, not at this stage. Unless you've been reported missing, I'd never find your name in my computer system, now would I? But I don't list badgers anyhow, not since the Reformation. Now, name, please?"

"Mesmer," Sabrina said before Salem could utter a word. "Austin Theobald Mesmer."

Type . . . type . . . type. . . . "Present whereabouts?"

Salem couldn't take it anymore. With a loud snort he cried, "If we knew that, we wouldn't be here!"

Mr. Chronis scratched at the stubble on his chin. "Maybe. Maybe not. You can't presume anything in this line of work."

"We don't know where he is, Mr. Chronis," Sabrina said, beginning to get annoyed herself. "That's what we're trying to find out."

"Where was he last seen?"

"He lived in a big mansion in Westbridge, a city in the mortal realm."

"W-E-S-T . . ." After several minutes of more slow typing, Mr. Chronis's computer gave a shuddering beep. "Nope," came the report. "No Mesmer listed. O'course, that doesn't mean he's not missing. It just means that nobody's filed a missing-persons report." He slid a form across his desk to Sabrina. "Here's the standard 12B-7CO5-A1. You can sit at the table over there and fill it out."

Sabrina studied the complicated form: height, weight, food preferences, shoe size, glasses prescription. "I don't know any of this stuff about Mesmer," she complained. "I just know his name."

"Then what do you wanna find him for?"

This time Sabrina had to keep *herself* from making a sarcastic comment. "It's a personal matter. Thanks for your help, Mr. Chronis, but I have to go."

"We badgers keep a tight schedule, you know," Salem added with a sneer.

As they hurried back to the linen closet, Sabrina said, "I guess there's only one thing I can do, Salem."

"And what's that?"

"Talk to the Keftiu again." This time, however, Sabrina intended to communicate with them more clearly. And to do that, she decided to blend in with the locals.

☆

Chapter 12

☆

Sabrina and dawn were not usually on intimate terms. The closest they'd come to meeting during the past few years was at a surprisingly well attended slumber party given by Valerie. Sabrina had been the last survivor of a decadent Friday night spent watching corny movies and gorging on popcorn and snack foods. Since all the other girls were snoring in most unladylike ways, it was left to her to turn off the TV and close the drapes. She remembered the sky out the window being a pearlescent shade that was fascinating, but she'd fallen asleep before the sun actually rose.

So much for natural phenomenon this time around. There was a lot of work to be done before school started, and that meant beating the sun up, or at least meeting it halfway. Sabrina wondered if she'd ever get a full night's sleep again.

The Spellman house was unnaturally quiet as she tiptoed through her dressing routine which, as usual, consisted of deciding what to wear and then zapping it on. She was sneaking down the stairs to grab a quick breakfast from the kitchen when she stepped on something warm and soft. It shrieked, and naturally, so did Sabrina.

"Hey! Watch the tail, willya?" Salem yelled as he scrambled out from under her feet.

"What are you doing on the stairs?" hissed Sabrina.

"Following the heat, of course," Salem said as if it should have been obvious. When Sabrina just stared at him, Salem explained, "Downstairs is warmest early in the night, but then it gets colder, so I keep moving up the steps until the heat runs out or the sun comes up, whichever happens first."

"I thought you were having a snuggle affair with Hilda's new down comforter."

Salem climbed up a couple of steps and settled on the runner. "It's still in the closet. She keeps it in there when she's not using it just to thwart me."

Sabrina realized what that meant. "You mean she didn't come back last night?"

"Nope, and neither did Zelda. That was some huff they went off in. Maybe they'll be gone as long this time as the last time."

"They've done this before?"

Salem gave a wicked kitty chuckle. "Once when they were mad at each other, they took off and blew right into a tornado, which spun them right over the rainbow and dropped them smack in Kansas. They were completely zapped out and had to pick corn for a week to earn bus fare back, heh-heh!"

A wave of guilt passed over Sabrina as she digested this information. She tried to ignore it. "Gosh, that would be too bad. But convenient." When Salem cocked an eyebrow at her, she hastily continued, "Well, they're the ones who've been ignoring me with that stupid Oil of Oblivion spell. I've got to zap myself to school really early today, and if they were here they'd just quiz me about what I was up to. But because of their spell, they wouldn't even hear my explanation, and so we'd end up going in circles until doomsday."

There was that word. *Doomsday.*

Sabrina shivered. "Salem, I gotta go." She raised her pointing finger.

"Wait!" Salem cried. "What about my breakfast?"

"Oh, go eat a bug," Sabrina grumbled, and with a zap, she was gone.

Salem gave a low growl. "Right. Then everybody will tell me I've got beetle breath."

It was cold in the maintenance building when Sabrina appeared there. Peering into the aquarium, she tried to make out the details of the villas clustered around an enthusiastically adorned forum complex. It was hard to tell, but she thought she could make out teeny weeny green forms in little groups. Some looked as if they were pruning the lichens and organizing gravel-shifting teams to tidy up the base of their mini-mountain.

Sabrina stepped back, closed her eyes, and concentrated as hard as she could. She had to. To pull this off right, she'd have to juggle several spells simultaneously, and that was hard for a novice witch.

The first spell she needed to cast was a combination shrink-and-sink-in-a-bubble spell as she had before. On top of that, she wanted to do a transmorph and stage her arrival with proper effects. After a moment of preparation, she opened her eyes again, gulped in a big breath of air, held it, and pointed at herself.

Everything flashed white.

No sooner did she register that she was now in the aquarium, afloat in an air bubble above the Keftiu forum, than the bubble shattered, sending billows of foam exploding all around her. For an agonizing instant her legs itched as if a thousand mosquitoes were having her for dinner, and then she found herself free-floating in the water.

All instincts told her to hold her breath, but Sabrina fought it down and forced her mouth open. Hesitantly she drew water into her modified lungs. She exhaled—or rather, spit. What a strange sensation! Although she was breathing water, oxygen was still reaching her lungs. She looked down to check out the rest of her transformation.

Her blond hair was now waist-long, and it floated in a cloud around her head, shimmering like golden kelp. Two big jewel-encrusted seashells and a massive number of pearl chains covered her essentials.

She still had a belly button, but that was where her human aspect stopped. Everything below the belt was all fish, one long-iridescent green tail covered in brazen scales that glinted in the faint morning light. Her caudal fin, as wide as the width of her spread arms, gently undulated in the current, and when she turned at the waist, she saw a long, shimmering dorsal fin that started at the base of her back and ended where her ankles used to be. Running a hand down her hip, she felt the slick, filmy texture of her scales, though if she tried to reverse the stroke, she almost cut her fingers on their sharp edges.

Oh, man, this is too cool! she thought. *I'm a mermaid!*

It took a moment to figure out how to move properly, but Sabrina finally isolated the muscles needed to flick her great tail back and forth. It was like having super-long rubber legs. She could bend her "knees" in both directions! She laughed aloud at the sheer delight of it, unaware that each flick of her powerful tail was propelling her upward. *It's like flying!* she thought, and was about to try a somersault when someone screamed. Then, two more someones screamed.

Alarmed, Sabrina turned to find four merchildren gawking at her. "Doom!" they shrieked in unison.

Oh, yeah, I'm not just a mermaid, Sabrina thought. *I'm a mermaid with a mission!* "Yes, I am the Conch Queen of Doom!" she proclaimed in the most doom-filled tone she could muster. She expected her voice to have a bubbly underwater quality, but to her ears, it sounded perfectly normal. With a surreptitious point of her finger, she surrounded herself with underwater lightning and ominous rumbles. Despite the gravity of the situation, it was kind of fun.

The merchildren shrieked in terror and darted away so fast she didn't even see them go. First they were there, then they were gone.

Sabrina looked around. "Hey, wait a minute! Come back!"

Amun Rahrah and his mermen came swimming around a bed of kelp and stopped short. "Halt or I'll—!" The captain of the merguard blinked in surprise. "Oh, it's you again."

"Oooooh, now is the time of trial and tribulation!" Sabrina rumbled. "I am the Conch Queen of Doom, come to warn you that Doom approaches! Great danger threatens you and all you hold dear!" She added a few more lightning strikes for effect.

Amun Rahrah's only comment was, "Make up

your mind, already! Last time you said you *weren't* Doom!"

Sabrina put her hands on her scaly hips. "I changed my mind, okay?"

A riot of excited voices approached, and Amun Rahrah's men surrounded Sabrina as a throng of curious Keftiu swam up from the city below. Sabrina decided it was time to pull out all the stops. With a series of quick finger points, she made lightning strike, thunder rumble, the current grow stronger, and a ghostly green light cast an eerie glow on the entire area. *I'm pretty good at this!* she thought.

Finally the Keftiu were properly impressed. The crowd scattered, and even some of Amun Rahrah's men backed away, unsure what to do. "I am the Conch Queen of Doom!" Sabrina howled again, magically amplifying her voice to give it a nice, chewy bass to press the point home physically.

The Keftiu murmured in awe at the only non-green mermaid they'd ever seen. Taking advantage of their hesitation, Sabrina leaned forward and kicked what used to be her legs with all her strength. "Whoa—!" she squealed as the powerful thrust sent her barreling forward faster than she expected.

Trying to remember all the mermaid cartoons she'd ever seen, she stretched her arms forward, then tilted them down, causing her whole body to make a long arc downward through the water. Still kicking her tail, she headed straight for the center of the city, every few moments remembering to shoot a bolt of lightning or make some thunder rumble. "I am the Conch Queen of Doom!" she kept repeating. The Keftiu she passed wailed in terror while the ones she'd left behind hurried to catch up.

Once inside the city Sabrina stopped in shock. The place was absolutely gorgeous! It was a maze of gently sloping streets, wide and pleasant, with lush plants and colorful sea-flowers waving lazily in the soft current. Houses and office buildings fashioned of clay and stone rose up around her, with graceful archways connecting them above for structural support. Keftiu certainly didn't need bridges, but they did need windows, and their buildings sported windows of every size and shape, each one revealing a colorful interior room beyond. *Wow, these guys may be whiners, but they definitely get an A-plus in architecture!*

That was when she heard the voices she'd been looking for. "You there, hold it!" came Ugawp's authoritative command. The leader of the Keftiu swam forward, flanked by his wife, Hyppshot, and the scroll-bearing Phinikas. All three eyed Sabrina with suspicion. "You're that bubble-girl from yesterday, aren't you?" asked Ugawp. "It was yesterday, wasn't it? You left before the argument really got started. When they called us for dinner, we looked up and you were gone. At least, I think it was dinner. Or was it lunch?"

"Yes," interrupted Sabrina, adding, "I am the

Conch Queen of Doom! Behold me now in my true form!"

Hyppshot turned to Phinikas and thrust out a wrinkled palm. "I was right, mackerel brain," she croaked. "Pay up."

"Not a clam," snorted Phinikas.

"What? You're backing out on a bet? You, the stickler for everything?" Hyppshot whirled on her husband. "Do you hear this, Ugawp? Yesterday I make a bet with him that she's the Conch Queen of Doom, even though she denied it, and now when she shows up saying she's the Conch Queen of Doom, your friend the Sage-Who-Knows-It-All won't pay up."

Ugawp avoided answering by scuttling behind his guards, leaving his wife and the Grand Vizier glaring at each other.

Sabrina felt her command of the situation deteriorating rapidly. "Prepare to fight for your lives!" she boomed ominously. "Doom is at hand!"

Phinikas shrugged. "Okay," he told Hyppshot, "I'll admit that she's a much more credible Conch Queen of Doom today than she was yesterday, the fins being a great improvement over those lumpy pink legs. But I do *not* accept that she's the right Conch Queen of Doom for us. I mean, she shows up and tells us—*tells,* mind you, not asks politely like a civilized supernatural apparition—that we must fight her Doom. What kind of Doom is it that you fight and avoid? Anybody who knows about Doom knows it's inevitable, right?"

Sabrina couldn't believe what was going on. "Didn't you hear what I said?" she barked at Phinikas. "I'm heralding the end of your race! Your city, your children, everything—*ka-blooey!* Aren't you going to do anything about it?"

That was the crux of her plan, after all. Sabrina figured that if she actually pushed the moment of Doom into their faces, the Keftiu would reveal some plan they had for escape, or some piece of information she could use to help them. She desperately hoped that they might even know of Mesmer's existence and be able to tell her where he might be. It was either that or, if Mr. Kraft had his way, their prophesied Doomsday would really come to pass.

Phinikas ignored her, however. He was listening as Hyppshot said, "You gotta point there. Just a point, and a little one at that, so don't let it go to your head." She jabbed a bony finger at Sabrina. "You, Goldie-Kelp. What's with this fighting and such like? Doom is Doom. Everything falls apart, the world comes to an end, everybody's unhappy, they're dead. It's bad news. That's why it's called Doom."

"You're wrong; he's right, Hyppshot," croaked Ugawp, finally gathering the gumption to contradict his wife. "This Conch Queen heralds the *wrong* Doom, and that's exactly what makes it the *right* Doom for *us.* You forget the wisdom learned by our ancestors—Things Get Worse.

It's only fitting that we should be destroyed for all time by the wrong Doom. Nothing's ever gone right for us before. Why should it start now that everything's going to end?"

"Let me get this straight," Sabrina said, straining to get a word in between rants. "You'll accept that I'm the Conch Queen of Doom, but you don't want to stop the Doom I'm warning you about?"

"Eh, so you're the Conch Queen of Doom, big deal," said Hyppshot. "You've done your job, you've warned us, blah blah. That's sweet. So now why don't you just go and leave us to meet our Doom? Oh, but don't forget to stop by the kitchen on your way out. They've got a seaweed soufflé today that'll melt in your mouth."

Out of sheer frustration Sabrina stabbed her finger upward. A wild explosion of lightning and thunder shrieked past overhead, sending shock waves of hot water slamming through the city. "Why won't you people do anything to save yourselves?" she yelled. "Do you want to lose everything that's important to you, including your *lives?*" Reflexively she tried to stamp her foot, but without feet to stamp, she only caused her caudal fin to twitch, sending her spiraling sideways. Quickly she righted herself, feeling like an idiot.

Fortunately the Keftiu weren't laughing. Then again, they weren't scared, either. "So what's new about losing the important things in life?"

Hyppshot was saying. "We've lost everything so often that we're champs. We've even lost the rest of the whole world, so losing our lives is a biggie? Please."

Sabrina tore at her hair. *"You people are enough to drive me crazy!"*

Then Ugawp said something that stopped all bickering dead. "The only thing we have ever lost that we truly regret is the Endless Waters."

Every merman and mermaid fell silent. All heads bowed. "The Endless Waters," they murmured in unison. "May we one day find our way back."

As if on cue, Phinikas fumbled to find a particular scroll among the dozen or so stuffed in his vest pockets. He found it and waved it over his head. "Is it not written that the Keftiu once abided in the Endless Waters, partaking of richness and pleasure and actually enjoying ourselves for once? But then we were driven out, and now exist within the boundaries of the Hard Water, which isn't so bad except it hurts to bump into. So says the Book of If-Only-We-Knew-Then-What-We-Know-Now."

Sabrina put two-and-two together. The Endless Waters . . . did they mean the ocean? And the Hard Waters . . . the walls of the aquarium? "Surely there must be some way to communicate beyond the Hard Waters?" she ventured, hoping they might give her a clue as to how much about the aquarium they actually knew.

"Only I speak to the Great Giant Face," said Ugawp, "but even it has abandoned us."

"The Great Giant . . . *Face?*" Sabrina said dubiously.

Amun Rahrah pointed to a blank wall of stone that stood in the town square at the far end of the street. "Upon the Sacred Wall we once beheld the Great Giant Face, whose mighty power made the plants grow and the food come. But it no longer shows itself, and we are alone."

Mesmer! Sabrina thought. *They must be talking about Mesmer! So he did communicate with the Keftiu—by posing as some sort of god!* Overjoyed at finally making some progress, she opened her mouth to ask the most important question: Did they know how to summon the Great Giant Face?

That was when an enormous hand tried to grab her.

Chapter 13

☆

The merpeople burst into bubbly screams and scattered as the giant hand reached down and grabbed several nearby trees. With a gargantuan tug, the trees were ripped free from the sea bottom in a storm of dirt and seaweed. Up they rose like limp green monsters, their roots flailing like withered arms until the giant hand lifted them beyond the water's surface and they disappeared.

"The Giant Hand has returned!" cried Ugawp. "We dared to dream of the Endless Waters, and now we're in for it, but good!"

Sabrina recognized the gold ring on one of the giant hand's fingers. "It's Mr. Kraft!" she wailed. "The one who'll bring your Doom if you don't listen to me—"

"No time, no time!" Hyppshot shrieked. "It's Doomsday! It's Doomsday! Hurrah!"

They're mad, Sabrina thought. But she knew she was wrong. The Keftiu weren't insane, just . . . confused about the facts. And at the moment they were in mortal danger.

"Get out of the way!" Sabrina shouted as Kraft's hand broke the surface high above and started another lethal descent. His fingertips were so huge that Sabrina could see every little loop and whorl of his fingerprints as if they were city streets. If she hadn't been swimming for her life, she might have been fascinated. As it was, she was too busy fleeing and trying to push Keftiu out of harm's way to notice much else.

She lost all bearings when she was yanked upward, tail-first, by the current created by Kraft's newest victim—a big, feather-leafed plant that dwarfed all the other "trees" in the area. Up she went, pulled along with several other Keftiu, dirt catching in her long seaweedy hair and bits of gravel the size of boulders whirling past her ears.

I've got to save the Keftiu! she thought desperately. *I can't let Kraft do this!* Kicking her caudal fin with all her might, Sabrina swam over to the nearest Keftiu, whose tail was tangled in the feather-tree's roots. She freed him, then managed to free another snagged Keftiu before the feather-tree broke the water's surface.

As if she were on some sickening amusement park ride, Sabrina's stomach did a serious flip as the dry world rose up around her. *I can't breathe!*

her mind shrieked. *I'm a fish now and I can't breathe out here anymore!*

Gasping and flailing, she clung to the feather-tree's roots, screaming silently when Kraft's nightmarishly huge face suddenly flashed past. She barely registered the manic glint in his billboard-size eyes when she realized she had to change back into a human being and fast!

She looked down and saw a bucket far below. It suddenly rushed toward her—Kraft had dropped her! Struggling to concentrate over the full-fledged panic rising in her throat, Sabrina pointed at herself and thought, *Revert! Revert! Revert!*

Mr. Kraft heard a strange banging sound and whirled around to find Sabrina Spellman standing behind him, soaking wet and with one foot in his bucket. Hugging herself against the cold, she smiled, then sneezed. "Hi, Mr. Kraft."

"What . . . ?" The word died on Kraft's lips. "How . . . ?" he tried again, with the same results.

Sabrina grabbed the opportunity. "Sure is cold in here," she said, and shuffled away, her foot dragging the bucket along with her. "Don't worry, I'll be right back. I just need to borrow your bucket." As she slipped through the door she added, "Oh, thanks for helping with the aquarium, but I think I can handle it from here, okay?"

Once she was out the door, she pulled her foot free and ran.

Mr. Kraft was many things: irritable, short-tempered, unsympathetic, sometimes even downright greedy—but he was not stupid. Often stupi*fied,* but not stupid.

Yet he felt like a complete ignoramus now. No matter how he tried, he just couldn't figure out what had happened in the maintenance room. How had Sabrina appeared like that? Why had she been wet? And what had she been doing with her foot in his bucket?

He'd decided it was all the fault of a new cola he'd been drinking. "O-D Cola: triple the sugar and triple the caffeine!" the bottle had said. Needing all the energy he could muster against the school epidemic, Kraft had guzzled a liter of it.

Now he was sorry he had. Obviously it had affected his mind.

As for the object of his worries—one Sabrina Spellman—she was no longer on the grounds of Westbridge High. Kraft had sent her home, and home she was, sitting in the Spellman house living room, brooding.

Sabrina couldn't believe her poor luck. Here she was home on a school day, declared sick yet perfectly healthy. She should be enjoying herself. After all, how many times does the VP send a student home when she's not sick? But, no, all

Sabrina wanted to do was go back to school! "Talk about having your priorities mixed up," she grumbled.

At least Zelda and Hilda hadn't returned yet from wherever their huff had taken them. If they'd been home, they'd have made her go back to school, and then Kraft would have made her go back home, and she'd have spent the rest of the day going back and forth and getting dizzy.

As it was, she couldn't stop thinking about the Keftiu. Yes, they were annoying. Yes, they were slightly . . . odd. But they were victims of a cruel fate, and Sabrina felt obligated to help them. But how?

She decided to try Zelda's approach: research the problem, and from that data, distill an answer. So she looked up the word *Keftiu* in the dictionary.

It wasn't there.

Next she went to the library and looked up "Keftiu" in the reference section. She came upon the word in an old cultural anthropology book. "'*Keftiu* was a Hebrew term used for the ancient Phoenicians,'" she read, "'and it also referred to peoples who traveled over the seas to settle on the Mediterranean coast.' Does that mean the Keftiu are ancient Phoenicians?" she wondered. "And if they are, how did they become mermaids?"

She remembered Hyppshot mentioning that her people had been desert dwellers before being turned into merfolk, but Hyppshot hadn't specified how or why they'd changed. And then Phinikas had said their city had sunk. And then Amun Rahrah had mentioned the Other Realm, but all he'd said was that the Other Realm had made things worse.

What did it all mean?

Sabrina returned home and, on a hunch, looked up *Keftiu* in *The Discovery of Magic*. Lo and behold, there it was—sort of. The entry read, "see Peoples, Lost and Found."

Sabrina slammed the book closed. "Great. Mr. Chronis again."

"Hi, Mr. Chronis." Sabrina waved at the old man, who was sitting at his desk, his face composed, hands neatly clasped before him, eyes closed. "Mr. Chronis?"

Nothing.

Sabrina moved cautiously forward. "Mr. Chronis?"

"Snnnnorrrrrr . . ."

Sabrina couldn't help but giggle. *He's asleep!* she thought, and then noticed the fine layer of dust on the old witch's shoulders. *My gosh, he must have been like this since I left last time!* Gingerly she reached out and tapped his arm. "Mr. Chronis?"

The old witch opened one eye. "No badgers allowed."

"What? Oh, Salem isn't with me today. Mr. Chronis, I need you to look up something for me."

"Not Mesmer again."

Sabrina was surprised that he remembered that. "No, this time it's the name of a race—the Keftiu."

Mr. Chronis hauled his frail form up out of his chair, and Sabrina could actually hear his joints creak as he shuffled over to a file cabinet. "Lost Peoples," he muttered. "Not on the computer yet." With a hard slap and a kick, he made the top drawer of the file cabinet pop open. "Spell it."

"K-E-F-T-I-U."

Faster than Sabrina would have thought possible, Mr. Chronis flipped through his files. "Anastasia . . . Earhart, Amelia . . . the Heckawee tribe . . . the Robinson family . . . no, went too far . . ." He grasped a thin file and yanked it up. "Here it is—Keftiu." He shuffled back to his desk, sat down, and opened the file. One piece of paper lay inside. Mr. Chronis skimmed it quickly, then looked up at Sabrina and stated, "Says here the K-E-F-T-I-U are the ancient peoples of the Lost City of Atlantis. Anything else I can help you with?"

Sabrina was somewhat confused by this turn of events. "But my aunts and I go to Atlantis all the time. It's not lost."

Mr. Chronis checked the list again. "You must be referring to the Found City of Atlantis. That is a whole different place."

"The Found City."

That was all she was going to get out of the old man. He had already returned to his snoring.

Sabrina's knees nearly buckled. She had found the legendary lost city of Atlantis in a fish tank, and Mr. Kraft wanted her to destroy it!

Chapter 14

☆

"Salem! Salem!"

Sabrina rushed out of the linen closet to find the cat asleep on the wicker clothes hamper on the second-floor landing—one of his usual afternoon resting spots. His head shot up, his eyes muzzy with sleep. "Huh—? Whu—?"

"Salem, wake up! You won't believe what I just found out!"

Salem blinked slowly. "That three left turns really do make a right?"

"No," Sabrina said. "The Keftiu are the lost people of Atlantis!"

"Really." Salem yawned. Then, *"Really?* The Lost City. I always wondered where they went."

"Yes, and Mr. Kraft wants me to destroy them!"

"Whoa, whoa, wait a minute." Salem slowly uncurled. "We cats can't properly assimilate

120

news until we're fully awake and properly stretched."

"Your eyes are open, you're awake," Sabrina snapped, and picking him up so that his hind legs dangled, she added, "And now you're stretched. C'mon, you've got to help me."

"Wait, how many times do I have to—?"

"Thanks, Salem!" Sabrina carried him downstairs to the kitchen. "Here's the problem. Mr. Kraft wants the Keftiu . . . er, the Atlanteans . . . well, their city, anyway . . . taken out of Mesmer's tank, but I can't move it because it's stuck to the bottom with a really strong magic spell."

"So move the whole tank," Salem suggested as Sabrina set him on the counter.

"I would, but I can't. Mr. Kraft wants to play boat games in it."

"Funny, he doesn't strike me as the nautical type."

"Salem!"

"Okay, I'm thinking, I'm thinking!" Salem thought. "Tell me this—if you *could* move the tank, where would you propose moving it *to?*"

"That's the tricky part." Sabrina paced back and forth across the kitchen floor. "The Keftiu—er, the Atlanteans—have legends about the Endless Waters where they lived after they were first turned into merpeople. They say they want to go back. So I was thinking"—and she spread her hands—"why don't I just send them back?"

"To the bottom of the ocean?" Salem asked dubiously.

"Yeah, why not?"

"It's awfully dark, for one thing."

"I'm sure they've got electric eels." Sabrina sat down, cradling her chin in her palms. "The problem is, I can't move them without using magic, and it won't be easy."

"Nothing worthwhile in life is easy," Salem drawled. "Except stealing leftovers from the trash can."

"Seriously, Salem, I've never done anything that big." Sabrina paused. "I've never done anything *half* that big."

"All right, let's break it down into manageable tasks." Salem sauntered over to Zelda's box of snack raisins and, butting it with his head, knocked it over. A pile of raisins fells out. One paw flick and Salem isolated a raisin to one side. "Raisin One," he said. "You have to move not only all the Atlanteans, but their city as well."

"That's a lot of little pieces to keep together," said Sabrina. "I remember what you told me about moving objects that belong together."

"Exactly. They don't stay together unless you concentrate on keeping them that way." Salem batted another raisin to one side. "Raisin Two: You'll have to move everything through space physically. No instant zapping this time."

"What? Why? It worked before."

"Think about it."

"What is this, cat, a test?"

"No, but it should be. You're messing around with real lives here."

Sabrina sobered up. "You're right." Her eyes narrowed in concentration. "I have to move everything physically through space because . . . because . . . I don't know!"

Displaying an unusual degree of patience, Salem prompted her, "What needs to happen when Atlantis reaches its destination?"

"It needs to stay there?"

Salem batted another raisin to one side. "No, it needs to be integrated with its new environment. It's easy to zap a lemon into a bathtub, but zapping an entire civilization into the ocean requires a delicate touch."

Sabrina wondered where in the world the cat had gotten the idea of a lemon in a bathtub, but it was a good analogy. A lemon was a self-contained object, like Atlantis had been the first time Sabrina had moved it. The castle, water and inhabitants had all been contained safely inside the tank as a single unit, like a lemon in its peel. This time Atlantis would have to be released from its peel, so to speak, to become part of the ocean environment. How could she keep the city intact and its citizens alive during such a maneuver?

Salem was already pushing another raisin with his paw. "And finally there's Raisin Four: You'll need to return the city and the people back to normal size."

That hadn't occurred to Sabrina. "Drat,

you're right. If the Atlanteans stay snack-size, they'll get gobbled up by who-knows-what before Hyppshot could even say 'Hurrah for Doomsday!' "

Salem cocked his head. "Come again?"

"Never mind." Sabrina thought of something else. "You know, I can't leave them in the tank anyway. If they have to expand back to normal size, they'll break the glass doing it. Somebody could get hurt."

"Well, there you go. So"—and Salem gestured with his paw—"here are four perfectly good 'raisins' why you have to remove Atlantis from the aquarium and physically transport it to the bottom of the ocean." With that said, he ate the raisins, explaining, "I need the fiber."

Sabrina slumped. "This all makes sense, Salem, except for one thing—I can't get Atlantis *out of the tank*. I already told you that." Suddenly the *boing* of a clever idea rang in her head. "Wait a minute! Maybe I *can*. . . ."

"That's it," urged Salem, chewing the sticky goo in his mouth. "For every impossibility there must be an equal and corresponding possibility. Or something like that."

Leaping to her feet, Sabrina said, "What if I just take the section of glass that Atlantis is stuck *to?* I'll ruin the tank, but I already warned Mr. Kraft there was a crack, right? All I need to do is enclose Atlantis in a bubble of tank water the same way I enclosed myself in a bubble of air. That way the Atlanteans and their city will survive a physical journey to the ocean and be free to expand when it gets there. Wow, I'm pretty smart! This will really work! Shouldn't it . . . ?"

Salem finished chewing and swallowed. "Ya got me. I've lost my ability to 'raisin' anymore."

For that, Sabrina almost lobbed the box of raisins at him.

☆

Chapter 15

☆

An hour later Sabrina stepped out of the linen closet and almost tripped because she wasn't looking where she was going. Instead her eyes were glued to the box in her hand. "What do you know? Aunt Hilda was right—the Other Realm Piggly Wiggly has everything."

"And at a substantial savings," Salem added, trotting out of the closet after her.

"That's only because you kept licking your chops and muttering *bacon* to our cashier. That's not a nice thing to say to a piglet. It was his first job."

"So sue me. It saved you a buck, didn't it?"

Sabrina ignored the cat and opened the box in her hands. Inside was a white device resembling a pocket calculator that beeped and booped when she aimlessly stabbed some of the buttons on its face. Opening up a little instruction booklet, she read, "'Congratulations! Now you can cast the most complicated, multilevel spells with the touch of a button using the new model Z44 Magical Macro Spell-Checker. Just preprogram each step of your spell into the Z44, using the Color Crystal system, and the Magical Macro Spell-Checker unit will coordinate and cast each phase of the spell for you, simultaneously or in a preprogrammed time sequence.' Sounds perfect." Sabrina started down the stairs. "What are we waiting for? Let's start programming!"

Hurrying into the dining room, Sabrina pressed a hidden button and watched as the dining room table flipped open to reveal Zelda's labtop. Rather like a portable laboratory in a box, the labtop always remained activated, even when it was closed up. Opening it revealed bottles and vials of liquid bubbling mysteriously over little Bunsen burners, while colorful fumes roiled through condensers. Neat rows of chemical ingredients in stoppered test tubes sat next to racks of pipettes, and on one edge a stack of petri dishes silently nurtured a variety of Other Realm chemical cultures. The slimy contents of one of the dishes wriggled like tiny worms, but Sabrina didn't even want to ask.

As Salem jumped up to the table, Sabrina upended the Spell-Checker box and poured a dozen cut crystals into her hand, each one as clear as a diamond. "These must be the patented Color Crystals," she said. "The instructions say I should preload each crystal with one sequence of the spell."

"Just remember to be specific," said Salem. "One sloppy prespell will ruin the whole thing."

"And I thought computers were bad. All right, then, I'll check my list." Sabrina pulled a folded piece of paper from her pocket on which she had written the list of spell sequences she'd need to move the Keftiu. "First, I need an Oil of Oblivion screen to make Atlantis invisible to mortals while I'm moving it."

Salem nudged a bottle into Sabrina's hand with his nose. "That's easy enough. Here's what's left of Zelda's and Hilda's formula."

"Great!" Sabrina dumped the bottle's gooey contents into a test tube, then added one crystal. "Now to add a drop of Spell-Bond . . ." Choosing a vial from the assortment in the labtop, Sabrina opened it and carefully tipped one drop of silvery liquid into the test tube. The resulting mixture flashed, and when the smoke cleared, nothing was left inside the test tube but the crystal, which now shone a brilliant blue.

"Now fit that crystal into slot number three," Salem instructed.

"Three?" Sabrina examined the Spell-Checker. Along the side of the device was a row of indentations labeled from 1 to 10. "If each slot is supposed to hold a preprogrammed crystal, why start with slot three? Shouldn't we start with slot one?"

"Nope," answered Salem. "Slots one and two have ROC's—Read-Only-Cantrips—to be used only if you want the Spell-Checker to operate in your absence or on a timed schedule."

"Oh." Sabrina studied the witch device with considerably more respect. "This thing is more complicated than I thought. How come you know so much about it?"

"I used one to conquer Ecuador. Worked like a charm."

Sabrina gave him a dubious look. "You conquered Ecuador?"

"I proclaimed myself king and ruled for an hour!"

"Just one hour? So what happened?"

"In an ongoing effort to fund my world-takeover plan, I economized whenever possible. I got a used Spell-Checker and found out too late that the Undo feature had a glitch. It would activate after an hour whether you wanted it to or not." His lip curled in annoyance. "Never stage a takeover using garage-sale equipment—they don't honor warranties."

Sabrina patted the cat's head. "An important lesson that I'll treasure forever. Now, can we get back to work?" She fitted the blue crystal into slot three, then consulted her list again. "Next I need to program a spell that's pretty complicated itself. To keep the Atlanteans alive while in transit, I have to encase their whole city in a water bubble that maintains all the conditions of the aquarium. You know, all that stuff Mr. Ichth told us about—water temperature, filtration, et cetera."

"Easy," Salem said. "Use that pamphlet Mr. Ichth gave you."

Sabrina's eyes lit up. "Perfect!" Then she frowned. "Now, where did I put it?"

It took her nearly ten minutes to find the pamphlet, which she'd stuffed into the pocket of the shirt she'd worn at the time, which she finally found at the bottom of her dirty clothes pile. Choosing the biggest test tube in the labtop selection, she rolled the pamphlet up and stuffed it in. Then she stuffed in another crystal and added a drop of Spell-Bond. *Poof!* The tube now contained a shiny green crystal programmed with all the information the pamphlet had contained. "Slot four?" Sabrina asked Salem.

"Slot four," he confirmed.

Sabrina fitted the crystal in and again turned to her list. "Oh, boy, this is going to take awhile. I've still got four whole programs to set."

"Refresh my memory."

Studying her list, she said, "Well, the basic transportation spell should be easy enough, I guess. I just have to make sure that Atlantis stays completely inside the water bubble as it floats. Then when it starts to sink down to the bottom of the Atlantic, I'll need a spell to equalize the water pressure between the bubble and the ocean so the poor Atlanteans don't pop. Then I'll need an enlargement spell combined with a sub-spell that will let ocean water seep into the bubble gradually, not all at once. It's got to be timed so that the second Atlantis is normal-size again, the water inside the bubble is the same as the outside. Then all that's left is an integration spell to make the city part of the ecosystem."

"Piece o' cake," Salem stated.

"For you, maybe," Sabrina retorted. "You're not responsible for all this."

"That's right, and I'm quite happy with that fact."

Sabrina gritted her teeth. Salem might be trying to help by maintaining a positive attitude, but flip answers only made her nervous. "But what if I make a mistake?" she moaned. "What if the bubble bursts, or the water pressure goes berserk, or a big shark eats the whole city before it has a chance to enlarge? Salem, one mess-up and I could go down in history as the witch who wrecked the legendary city of Atlantis!"

"All I have to say is—better you than me."

Sabrina gulped. "Thanks, cat."

Chapter 16

☆

A short time later, Sabrina stood in front of the aquarium, the Spell-Checker clutched in her hand. She raised her pointing finger, then stopped. "Drat! I have to coordinate a bunch of spells just to go down there again." She glanced hopefully at the Spell-Checker, but knew better than to mess with its programming at this point.

Then inspiration struck. Pointing at herself, she chanted,

"Remembering spells is a really big bore;
Just cast all the spells that you cast before."

A flash of light, a bubbly explosion of air, a tingling of the legs, and suddenly Sabrina the tiny mermaid was floating in the aquarium again. "I could get to like this," she said, enjoying the wonderful sensation of weightlessness. Then, with more control this time, she flicked her dorsal fin and propelled herself downward into Atlantis.

"Halt or I'll—you *again?*" came Amun Rahrah's voice. He and his merguard surrounded her before she could say a word. "What kind of Conch Queen of Doom are you?" he griped, angrily jabbing at Sabrina with his trident. "First you lie about your job, then you declare Doomsday, but do we get destroyed? Nooooooo, just mucked around with by the Giant Hand. The town square's a mess, uprooted trees are everywhere, and now here you are again! What are you doing this time, delivering a plague of lobsters?" He didn't give Sabrina a chance to answer. "You're coming with me, Conch Queen of Doom. The Maav-En is going to have something to say to you!"

"Perfect," said Sabrina cheerfully. "I've got something to say to him. Lead on."

Confused but determined not to show it, Amun Rahrah's men herded Sabrina down to the city's street level. They swam through the downtown section, weaving between restaurants and beauty shops and clothing stores and museums until they came to city hall. Sabrina tried to marvel at the exquisite architecture, but Amun Rahrah kept hustling her onward, faster, as if he wanted to keep her off balance. *He's just doing his job,* she thought calmly as she was guided down a corridor and up into a private office. *I guess he's got a right to be suspicious of me.*

Amun Rahrah rapped once on a door marked with a seashell sign in a carved coral frame. Sabrina couldn't read the words. They looked like Greek to her, and for all she knew, they really *were* Greek. But obviously it was the office of Ugawp, because from inside, the Hereditary Maav-En, Sitter on the Clamshell Throne and Intermediary to the Great Giant Face, yelled, "Come in, already! I could go deaf with all that rapping."

The door opened and Sabrina was escorted in.

"The Conch Queen of Doom!" yelped Hypp-shot. She was floating behind the desk at Ugawp's left. Phinikas floated to the Maav-En's right.

Sabrina decided she had to take control of the situation right away, before the Keftiu could start bickering about anything. "I have come to save you!" she declared.

The merfolk did a double-take. "You having an identity crisis or something?" asked Phinikas. "First you weren't the Conch Queen of Doom, then you were, now you're saying you're a rescuer? Maybe you should talk to a good job counselor."

"I wasn't, then I was, and now I am," Sabrina said. "I mean, it's just that now I have a way for you to survive your Doom." She held up the Spell-Checker. "See?"

Hyppshot squinted at it. "What is that, a sandwich?"

"It's not time for lunch yet, is it?" asked Ugawp. "I just had breakfast. Or was that dinner?"

"It's not a sandwich!" said Sabrina. "This is the, uh . . . Magical Box of the Endless Waters. With it, I'm going to send you back there, all of you, and your whole city, where you can live happily." *If that's possible,* she thought to herself.

The Keftiu looked skeptical. As well, they looked confused, but not because of what Sabrina had said. Ugawp's comment about food had them all scrambling to find their personal schedules to see what meal it was.

"I'm serious," said Sabrina. "Wouldn't you like to go? I mean, it's what you talked about before—how much you wanted to go back to the Endless Waters."

"Promises, promises," Phinikas muttered, busily checking the schedule he'd found.

"How do we know you speak the truth?" asked Ugawp, snatching the schedule away from the Grand Vizier and peering at it in confusion. It was upside down.

For lack of any other evidence, Sabrina waved the Spell-Checker. "I have this."

"And I have heartburn when I eat the wrong meal," said Hyppshot in a dismissive tone.

"No, really, listen, please." Sabrina lowered

the Spell-Checker and tried to speak as sincerely as she could. "I mean this. I can send you back to the Endless Waters. You don't have to meet your Doom. Not today, anyway. Just take me to the center of your city, and I'll prove it."

The three old merpeople glanced at one another, each curious to see if his or her fellows would take the bait. Finally Phinikas pulled a scroll from his vest pocket and opened it up. "As it says in the Book of Would-I-Lie-to-You?, 'He who lives by suspicion is paranoid, but who knows—it might be true.' Let's give it a try, what the heck we got to lose?"

Ugawp and Hyppshot solemnly nodded in agreement.

Sabrina held back a whoop of joy. *They agree on something!* she thought with glee. *Miracles* do *happen! They finally agree on something!*

The merfolk guided her out of the building and back into the streets. A quick swim around the block and Sabrina found herself in the town square, right in front of the Sacred Wall she'd heard about earlier. As Amun Rahrah had said, the square was a mess, with uprooted trees and mounds of upturned seabed everywhere, but cleaning crews had already tidied a good portion of it. Amun Rahrah dispersed the workers with an impatient wave of his trident.

"Where is the exact center of the city?" Sabrina asked. "It has to be precise."

Ugawp pointed to a podium that stood near

the Sacred Wall. "There. That is where I used to confer with the Great Giant Face."

Sabrina swam over to the podium. A crowd of citizens was gathering, their expressions a mixture of awe, curiosity, and skepticism. Sabrina ignored them and concentrated on the Spell-Checker. *Here goes nothing,* she thought. *Or rather, here goes* everything!

She pressed the button.

In the maintenance room of Westbridge High School, no one was present to see the Mesmer aquarium begin to shake. The glass sides of the tank trembled and wobbled as if they were melting, and suddenly they disappeared. But no water spilled. No fish tumbled to the floor. No gravel fell into piles. The water inside the tank magically pressed in on itself and held its contents in place. As one unit it rose upward, forming a ball the size of a picnic table within which the city of Atlantis sat serene and whole, still stubbornly attached to its section of tank bottom.

The ball of water glided through the air like a giant raindrop that refused to fall. It headed for the maintenance room window, which was open, and sailed out into the afternoon sunlight.

As programmed, the city of Atlantis took the most direct route to the Atlantic—straight east. Unfortunately, this took it right through the center of Westbridge High's main facilities. It entered through an open door and floated down a corridor, past students and teachers who remained oblivious to its presence. It barely missed hitting Harvey's arm, and would have splooshed right into Libby's face had she not suddenly bent over to tie her shoelace. It turned a corner, floated down that hallway, turned another corner, and headed right for Mr. Kraft.

The magic of Sabrina's spell urged Kraft to step aside, but the VP was preoccupied with a paper in his hand, so he continued straight forward, oblivious to the globe of water heading for him. It did not veer from its path and so struck his shoulder, soaking his jacket and shirt and causing the words "What in blazes—?" to fall from his lips.

But that's all he said, because Mr. Kraft was now soaking wet without any rational explanation for it. As he stood there spluttering and gaping in shock, the ball of water carried Atlantis out another door, over the lawn, through the student parking lot, and out into the city of Westbridge. Once free in the open air, it picked up speed. Ten minutes later it hovered over the Atlantic Ocean.

Sabrina couldn't help but worry. By now the merpeople knew something weird was happening. They'd all made their way to the center of the city, and the cacophony of voices was unbelievable, with everyone commenting on every little change around them. It was like listening to a symphony of voices with no conductor at the helm.

Of course, no one could actually see the outside world as it passed by. Still, no matter what direction they looked, the merpeople saw strange wavering images—objects and colors that almost made sense, but which were too distorted by water to recognize clearly. For that, Sabrina was grateful. She remembered what it had felt like to see Mr. Kraft's face two hundred feet tall. A few hundred Keftiun nervous breakdowns would have been too much for her to handle.

The Spell-Checker beeped, signaling Sabrina that the fourth crystal had completed its programming. That meant that Atlantis was just about to drop into the Atlantic Ocean. "Okay, everybody, we're almost there," she told the merpeople. "Hold on!"

Atlantis shook as the globe of water pushed down into the ocean, defying normal gravitational laws and pulling the tiny city downward until it rested on the ocean floor. Then Sabrina got the distinct impression that she was growing, even though everything around her remained the same. Her arms and fin felt like taffy being stretched, and the weirdest part of all was that it didn't hurt. *We're enlarging,* she thought, giddy with pleasure at her success thus far.

Her mermaid senses detected a change in the water chemistry. It tasted different, more tangy now, with a subtle bitterness that made her tongue curl. It wasn't bad, particularly—more like drinking tap water from a different part of the country for the first time. The temperature of the water dropped, then rose again and stabilized, and a current of spicy water flowed past, carrying smells and tastes so foreign that Sabrina couldn't have described them if she'd wanted to.

The Spell-Checker emitted a long beep. All sequences had been completed. Atlantis was home.

Beaming with pride, Sabrina watched as the Keftiu slowly swam upward, gawking over the roofs and towers of their city at the new world around them. Atlantis itself was the same as ever, but they knew darned well that everything else had changed. For one thing, there were more fish swimming around, fish the Keftiu had never seen before. Whole schools of little flashing bodies darted past, executing complex paths through the water as if they were dancing. High above, huge shadows loomed past, suggesting massive creatures—whales, Sabrina guessed, probably species the Keftiu had never heard of. It was hard to see them distinctly because it was much darker now. "You may need to put up some streetlights," she said happily. "So what do you guys think?"

Ugawp, Hyppshot, and Phinikas floated together, each of them looking in a different direction. Then they all turned to Sabrina and frowned. "We hate it!" they grumped in unison.

Chapter 17

☆

W HAT?" blurted Sabrina.

"It's cold," complained Ugawp. "Why is it so cold?"

"It's like night down here," Phinikas snapped. "Who wants to live in a constant midnight? We're merfolk, not vampires."

"Hey, look down here!" somebody else called from below. "The gravel's gone! It's all muddy! This'll be impossible to keep clean!"

A little mergirl pulled strands of a plant out of her hair. "Ick, this stuff is gross!"

A young merwoman swatted at some small fish darting around her head. "These rotten little things are like gnats!" she snarled.

Hyppshot peered into a grove of sea plants and came face to face with a shark. She shrieked like a banshee and fled, and all the other merpeople saw the shark, shrieked like banshees and fled after her.

Sabrina couldn't argue with this, so she fled, too, trying not to shriek. The shark made a lazy snap at a merman, then simply swam away.

Sabrina found the entire population of Atlantis crowded together in a park down the street. "That's it!" yelled Ugawp. "We're not staying here! It's a death trap!"

"Death trap, death trap!" the merpeople chanted, and then everybody began to complain. Fueled by their recent scare, they yelled so hysterically that their complaints sounded like the squawking of excited chickens.

Sabrina tried to calm them down, using magic to amplify her voice. "Don't worry, everybody! You just have to get used to the changes! It's nice down here, honest! These are the Endless Waters you wanted! All kinds of creatures live together down here, and you'll learn to get along with them, too! This is where you belong, you said it yourself, remember?"

Predictably, the Keftiu ignored her—until the ground shook. That got their attention. They stopped complaining and began to scream again. "It's Doomsday after all!" shouted Hyppshot. "Hurrah!"

"Hurrah!" chorused the crowd.

A voice like thunder came out of nowhere, roaring through the city like a freight train: "Not *you* again! No! NO!"

The seabed shook harder.

The merpeople collapsed into chaos. Between screams they complained, and between complaints they screamed. The seabed bucked and heaved, creating pulses of water that threw everybody off balance first one way, then the other. And in the middle of all this, Sabrina the mermaid floated, so stunned and disappointed she could hardly react anymore. By nature, she was not a quitter, but at this particular moment, she could think of no other course of action. No matter what she had tried to do, the Keftiu had hated it. Now the sea itself was freaking out.

She threw her Spell-Checker away and hugged herself, as if trying to find comfort in her own convictions. "I only tried to help them!" she shouted to herself as the roar of the seaquake grew louder. "I only tried to help!"

"Look!" howled Phinikas, and pointed. Sabrina turned to see the Sacred Wall over in the town square light up. The face of an old man appeared, and he looked down the street into the park where the merpeople were gathered.

The seaquake stopped.

Everything grew quiet.

"It's the Great Giant Face!" crowed Hyppshot. "We've been saved!"

The Keftiu chattered with relief, but were instantly silenced when the Great Giant Face spoke. "YOU, MAID."

Sabrina pointed at herself. "Who, me?"

"YES, YOU," said the Great Giant Face. "COME. WE NEED TO TALK."

The next thing Sabrina knew, her mermaid form had vanished and she was once again a normal girl standing on dry land—or rather, a carpet, one that luxuriously covered the floor of what appeared to be a huge private library. Tall ornate bookshelves carved from polished mahogany covered most of the wall space, their shelves neatly stuffed with hundreds—thousands—of books. Paintings filled the spaces between the bookcases, and an authentic medieval tapestry hung from ceiling to floor at one end. The entire room held only one other piece of furniture: an antique writing desk with chair.

A pleasant yellow sun-glow streamed in from the casement window, a warm breeze billowing the soft, gauzy curtains, casting filmy shadows against the walls. Beyond the window, Sabrina could see an expansive lawn and garden that looked vaguely familiar.

The man who stood at her side was also familiar. For one thing, he was the Great Giant Face. And as he stared curiously at her, Sabrina's memory suddenly snapped the facts into place. "You're Mesmer!" she blurted.

Chapter 18

☆

☆

Well, of course I am! Who else could I possibly be?" Professor Austin Theobald Mesmer puffed out his chest and regarded Sabrina as if she were a foolish child who couldn't recognize the obvious if she tripped over it. His pale green eyes narrowed as he scrutinized her face. He squinched up his apple cheeks and pursing his pudgy lips. "Now the question is, who are *you?*"

Sabrina couldn't speak. After the events of the last two hours, she was so confused that she wasn't sure what species she was anymore. Finally she crowed, "You're not dead!"

Mesmer knitted his brows, worried. "Am I supposed to be?"

"Yes! I mean, *no,* not at all. Wait, I'm sorry," Sabrina spluttered, finally getting a grip. "It's just that I've been trying to find you. Everybody thinks you're dead, but I know you're a witch. I guess you figured out that I'm a witch, too. Well, a half-witch, actually. My mom's a mortal. Have you had Atlantis in your fishtank for long?"

Mesmer's expression softened. "For millennia," he said. "And I'll have them for millennia more, until every grain of Time has passed through the hourglass of all creation." He broke out into a wide grin. "Say, that was pretty good, wasn't it? I studied rhetoric under Aristotle, you know. But back to business. I don't know how you discovered my little secret, Miss, um, um——"

"Sabrina Spellman."

"Sabrina Spellman, my curiosity is piqued. What were you doing? The Keftiu don't take kindly to witches. In fact, I'd go so far as to say they hate us. Then again, they've got reason to, I suppose."

Sabrina remembered her first visit with the fussy fish people. "I'm not sure they particularly hated me, but they did think I was the bringer of all death and destruction."

Mesmer snorted, as if to say, *Well, there you are.*

"But I was only trying to help," Sabrina continued. "Professor Mesmer, they didn't know they were in a fish tank. Why not?"

"That, my dear, is a long story, a very long story indeed." Mesmer leaned tiredly against his writing desk. "Forgive me, but I'm a bit fatigued. I was sunbathing off the coast of Fiji when I heard Leviathan roar. Needless to say, I returned with the utmost haste." He patted his chest as if congratulating his heart for a job well done. "Whoo, haven't moved that fast in centuries!"

"Huh?" was all Sabrina could think of to say.

Mesmer waved at the chair behind the writing desk. "Have a seat, my dear. I'll explain everything."

Sabrina sat down. "So . . . you're not mad at me?"

"Mad? At you? Oh, my, heavens, no," Mesmer assured her, amused at the notion. "Actually, you've done me a favor. You see, the Keftiu are very difficult. That's why I'm their keeper. But, please, let me begin at the beginning."

As Sabrina settled herself comfortably, Mesmer's tone changed to that of a professor addressing a class of attentive students. He grasped the lapels of his coat and declared, "I'm old, as you might guess, even for a witch. I walked the sands along mortal realm beaches when mankind still wore animal skins and lived in caves. The fate of the Keftiu was placed in my hands millennia ago, and for all these years, I have executed my duties with the utmost care and devotion." His tone suddenly turned casual. "But, goodness gracious, even I need a vacation once in a while. The Witches' Council allows me a seven-year absence once every thousand years."

"A seven-year absence," Sabrina murmured. "It all fits!"

A guilty expression crossed the old witch's face. "At this point in my life, I'm used to coming and going as I please. But since my last vacation, the laws of the mortal realm have changed. Nowadays, if someone disappears for more than a few *days,* the authorities step in. I simply didn't realize that my entire estate, and with it the Keftiu, was in danger."

"So how did they end up in a fish tank?" Sabrina asked. "I mean, until I learned that I was a witch on my sixteenth birthday, I didn't even know that Atlantis was real. But this isn't the same Atlantis that I've been to."

"I assume that you are referring to the Atlantis resort. Sometimes people jokingly refer to it as the 'found city.' I will get to that in a moment. As for the Keftiu, there are many realities that remain unknown to mortals, my dear. The Keftiu are among them, and for a very good reason, a very good reason indeed." Mesmer paused, carefully choosing his next words. He finally had to put it this way: "The fact is, they're a pain in the posterior."

Sabrina laughed. "That's one way of putting it."

"That's the only way of putting it. The Keftiu are in a fish tank because they can't get along with anyone. They never could, and I doubt they ever will. You see, their race originated in the Other Realm—"

"You mean they're witches?"

"No," Mesmer corrected her, "but there is

something magical about them. They're unusually artistic, for one thing. Mortals consider the ancient Greeks to have set the standard for many of the classic arts, but the Keftiu surpass the Greeks by far." He nodded to himself. "Oh, yes, far by far."

Sabrina thought of the city, remembering the graceful architecture of the buildings, the lush landscaping on the hillsides, the tranquil aura of the city streets. Even the Keftiu themselves had a classic beauty about them—their hair, their clothes, the way they moved. They were like ballet dancers in water. "What a shame they're so whiny," she concluded. Then she realized she'd said it aloud. "Oh, I'm sorry!"

"Bosh," said Mesmer flatly. "You've hit the proverbial nail on its proverbial head. The Keftiu don't like *anything*. All they do is complain and bicker with one another, and they've been preoccupied with their own doom for nearly five thousand years. They argue about it constantly—how it will happen, when it will happen, the signs of its happening . . ." He shuddered. "Eventually the witch community just couldn't stand them anymore. The entire city was banished to the mortal realm, transported here by the Witches' Council of that time, who put it near Egypt. For an ancient mortal race, the Egyptians were surprisingly tolerant.

"But it took a mere six months for the Keftiu to drive them crazy. The Pharaoh begged his gods to destroy them, so the Witches' Council

149

stepped in and did the next best thing—they transported the whole city to an island, oh, let me see . . . yes, it was in the Ionian Sea, between Sicily and Crete. But it didn't stay there long. The Keftiu's constant whining scared visitors away, all but ruined the local tourist trade. As you can imagine, the Sicilians weren't happy about this and prepared for war, so the Witches' Council stepped in again." Here Mesmer heaved a heavy sigh. "My dear, every place the city was relocated became a war zone. At one point it was even moved to Antarctica, but the penguins— usually very pleasant—couldn't stand the bickering, either. They became hostile and the Keftiu had to be rescued. Can you imagine? Rescued? From *penguins?*"

Try as she might, Sabrina just couldn't imagine it. She'd seen a lot of bizarre things since becoming a witch, but a murderous hoard of angry penguins proved a strain even for her.

"Well, finally it was decided that the Keftiu city should be relocated out in the Atlantic," said Mesmer. "The city was named Atlantis in the hope that a new identity might help its reputation, clean the slate, so to speak." His eyes grew misty with memory. "Atlantis, oh, what a beautiful place! It didn't take long before it was world famous. Vacationers came by the droves, and merchant sailors went out of their way to make it a port of call. But the Keftiu remained the same. Their complaining ruined their new reputation in no time. Believe me, my dear, when a sailor prefers to stay out at sea rather than put into port, you know that port has got to be bad.

"By now the Keftiu were convinced that everybody hated them—and they were right. So the Witches' Council made one last attempt to find them a home. They sank the entire island to the ocean bottom so that no one would ever have to deal with them again."

Sabrina jumped to her feet. "That's when they were changed into mermaids!"

Mesmer nodded. "They were magically integrated into the ocean environment and left to fend for themselves. The plan worked, too. The Keftiu may be whiners, but they're survivors. They learned to love the ocean and soon preferred their merbodies over land bodies. But again"—and Mesmer's shoulders slumped— "they ruined it. Even fish have ears, after all, and all the whining and bickering soon drove them away. Even the kelp left, riding the currents to less troubled waters. Leviathan, the great guardian of the sea, demanded that the Witches' Council do something once and for all to rid the mortal realm of what he termed 'the most annoying race ever to evolve.'"

"So they got put in a fish tank," Sabrina finished, finally understanding. "Sad but clever."

Mesmer waggled his fingers in a maybe-yes-maybe-no gesture. "It worked, true, but it required deception on the council's part. The

Keftiu have no idea where they are, not only for their own protection but for their self-esteem as well."

That made sense to Sabrina. If she knew one thing from being a teenager, it was the need to belong and be liked—the primary goal of all teenagers. No wonder the Keftiu had such a prophecy of Doom. Their whole history was fraught with rejection and disaster. Even if they deserved every bit of it, it was still hard not to feel sorry for them.

"Of course," Mesmer continued, "the Witches' Council regretted the decision immediately. They lost one of their favorite vacation spots. To compensate they built the Atlantis Resort, which you mentioned earlier."

"So you're the Keftiu Keeper now?" she asked Mesmer.

He nodded. "An aquarium is a complete bio-environment, but it is not self-sustaining. I was appointed to look after the Keftiu for all Time."

"I'm so sorry," Sabrina said, and she meant it. "I just tried to help them once, and my life has been a mess ever since." She told Mesmer about Kraft's plans for the Westbridge High School Augmented Studies Department, which was supposed to become the cornerstone of the Willard H. Kraft Learning Center. Mesmer listened attentively as Sabrina told him everything, from her first visit to the estate to Kraft's plans for the modified fish tank.

"And this man has been appointed to teach

children how to think?" Mesmer said of Kraft when she finished.

To her surprise, Sabrina came to the VP's defense. "He doesn't know he's hurting anybody, Professor Mesmer. He's just trying to do a good thing for the school, just as I was trying to help the Keftiu."

That made Mesmer smile, one of those *isn't she cute?* smiles that parents give their children when they do something praiseworthy. "And I think you were an angel to try, my dear, but as you know now, the Keftiu cannot be helped. Their nature is to complain, and no matter what their circumstances, that's what they'll do. If you ask me, I think they enjoy it."

Sabrina thought back to the seaquake. "Somebody sure *doesn't* enjoy it. I meant to ask, whose voice did I hear down there? It sounded like a monster movie soundtrack in Dolby stereo."

"That, my dear, was Leviathan. A long memory, he has. He caused the seaquake you experienced out of anger at the return of Atlantis, and he would have kept the sea quaking until the Witches' Council took the city away." The old witch suddenly headed for the door. "Follow me. I have something to show you."

Sabrina trailed Mesmer out into the hallway, down two flights of stairs, and through a double door. Before them stretched a hallway that Sabrina recognized—the portrait hall containing all the paintings of Mesmer's ancestors. "It must be fascinating to be able to trace your ancestry back so far," she commented as they passed the line of historical faces.

"Don't be silly," said Mesmer. "Those are all me."

Sabrina felt like an idiot. Of course! Mesmer was his own ancestors! He'd been existing in the mortal realm for centuries and so had been forced to create his own family line in order to pose as a mortal. Sabrina wondered how many names he'd had, how many lives he'd lived, how much of human history he had influenced. All witches were morally bound not to tamper with mortal history, but still, even the most conscientious witch had to become part of his or her chosen environment just to survive. And Mesmer had survived an awfully long time.

The old witch led her into the aquarium suite, and Sabrina's jaw dropped. There, sitting in the middle of the floor on its pedestal, was the enormous aquarium complete with Atlantis, all arranged as it had been when Sabrina had first seen it. The filtering system had been restored, and all the tubes that Sabrina had inadvertently cut were whole again, snaking their way through the holes, down to the elaborate Other Realm equipment below. "H-how did you bring it back so fast?"

"I didn't," said Mesmer. "The council did. I contacted them the moment I heard Leviathan's roar. The council rescued the Keftiu while I attended to you."

Mesmer walked slowly around the aquarium,

one hand raised, his fingertips lightly brushing the glass as he moved. For all of his remarks about the Keftiu being annoying, Sabrina could tell that he was very fond of them. "Everything looks fine," he concluded, after staring into the depths for several minutes from different angles. "Doubtless the Keftiu are shaken up, but it will give them something new to complain about." He met Sabrina's gaze. "Would you like to say goodbye to them?"

The question sparked a series of memories in Sabrina's mind: the glorious sensation of floating underwater versus the terrifying sensation of suffocating at the hands of a gargantuan Mr. Kraft; the cool brush of seaweed hair against her neck versus the rumble of a seaquake beneath her fins; the splendor of touching a legendary city versus the torture of hearing constant whining and whining and more whining . . .

Mesmer noted her hesitation. "My dear, you are probably the last outsider they will ever see, except for me. I created the concept of the Sacred Wall only so that I could communicate when absolutely necessary. I'm sure they'd want to see you again."

"Maybe." Sabrina spiraled her hands, groping for words. "I don't know . . . I think the Keftiu have been through enough. Another visit will just freak them out. Besides, I've got to get home. It's late." She could tell by the angle of the light filtering in through the window that the sun was going to set soon. Her aunts would be wondering where she was . . . if they weren't totally oblivious of her existence now, that is.

"Very well," said Mesmer. "But you deserve one last look." Pointing his finger, he made a Looky Loop appear in the air next to the aquarium. A few mumbled words, and he gestured for Sabrina to take a look. "I think you'll be pleased."

Curious now, Sabrina peered through the Looky Loop and found herself watching a crowd of Keftiu in their town square. Amun Rahrah was there, holding the merfolk back from a large object covered with a seaweed tarp. Ugawp and Hyppshot were making some kind of speech, complete with hand waving and fist shaking, and when they finished, they turned to Phinikas, who raised his hands. No doubt he was quoting something. Then, with a flourish, two mermen pulled away the seaweed tarp to reveal a statue.

"Hey, it's me!" Sabrina squealed in surprise. "No, wait a minute. *Is* that me . . . ?"

Mesmer gazed into the Looky Loop as Sabrina continued to study the tiny statue standing in the center of the mini mercity. It was a tall, lumpy thing, but it definitely had arms and what could have been a mertail. Long golden seaweed floated from the top of what must have been a head. That is, it looked kind of like a head, with two blobby spots that might have been eyes and a wide hole that, uncomplimentary enough, looked like a mouth. The whole thing was the same shade that Sabrina's merbody had been.

"I thought you told me that the Keftiu were superior artists," Sabrina said to Mesmer. "You sure? That statue looks like a deformed snowman after a long rain."

Mesmer was scratching his head, as if that would help him come up with an explanation. "Hmm. Perhaps they're not so good in the arts anymore. I don't know, maybe the pH is off. . . ."

Chapter 19

The following Monday morning, Sabrina, Harvey, and Valerie walked briskly across the Westbridge High School quad. Mr. Kraft strode ahead of them, flanked by the members of the District School Board, who were then followed by PTA members, some of the faculty members, and then school staff. Sabrina, Harvey, and Valerie came next, along with the rest of the Mesmer Team.

Desmond Jacobi had finally recovered from his spots and come back to school, much to Kraft's relief. Sabrina found great satisfaction in watching the jock flinch whenever Gordie got too close to him. "I wonder what disease he had," Valerie said, watching him. "I mean, all those spots. Gross."

"Tell me about it," came Libby's voice. Sabrina turned to find the cheerleader walking behind her, staring daggers at Dez's back. "I'm not keen on tagging after the freak brigade, but at least you three don't break out in spots."

"Ya never know," Sabrina said cheerfully.

Libby shot her a glare and purposefully slowed down, putting more space between them. "How true," she agreed primly.

Harvey pointed toward the school's guest parking lot. "Say, Sabrina, aren't those your aunts?"

Sure enough, Sabrina turned to see Zelda and Hilda getting out of their car—and Professor Mesmer was with them!

"Who's the fossil?" Valerie asked.

"That's Mesmer," answered Sabrina. "He's really nice."

"Did your aunts know him before or something?" Harvey asked. "You sure have gotten close since he turned up."

Chuckling, Sabrina explained, "Let's just say we've got a lot in common."

Valerie leaned close. "Lucky for you. If you hadn't made that deal with Mesmer, Kraft would have put you on permanent detention."

The "deal" hadn't been Sabrina's doing. It hadn't even been her idea. Mesmer had contacted Mr. Kraft to announce his return. Kraft had been mortified to think that the school would lose its donations, but then Mesmer had credited Sabrina for convincing him to let West-bridge High permanently keep all the items they'd borrowed.

At that, Kraft became ecstatic, to say the least, though once again, strange occurrences had involved Sabrina Spellman. When Sabrina herself couldn't adequately explain how she'd found the millionaire, and Mesmer refused to speak of it, Kraft had become very suspicious. Fortunately, all he really cared about in the end was his dream of the Willard H. Kraft Learning Center, which he was sure would become a reality now.

As for the aquarium itself, Mesmer had taken care of that, as well. After she'd seen the Keftiu safely returned to Mesmer's mansion the week before, Sabrina had returned to school to discover that Mr. Kraft—wearing a surgeon's mask to protect himself from Des's nonexistent virus—was looking for her. He'd immediately escorted her over to the maintenance building and pointed at the aquarium—the aquarium that shouldn't have been there anymore. "How did you do that?" he had demanded.

"That" had turned out to be a pristine aquarium, exactly like the original one but minus the Keftiu and all the fish. In fact, this aquarium was all set up for Kraft's first naval battle reenactment, the 1805 battle at Cape Trafalgar, complete with model ships.

Being a very powerful witch, Mesmer had been able to cast a spell that gave Sabrina "exactly what she needed." Kraft had been flabbergasted at how fast Sabrina had converted the aquarium, and he was also angry that she had neglected to order plastic containers from him. But he loved the results, and was especially pleased that Sabrina had managed to fix the crack in the aquarium that had never been there at all.

All in all, events had sorted themselves out, and Sabrina felt on top of the world. Now all she had to do was endure this presentation and her life would go back to being normal again.

Well, as normal as it could be for her, anyway.

She entered the school maintenance building to find the aquarium lit with theatrical lights, very dramatic, very impressive. To one side, the school video club had set up a camera to capture the mini-battle for future viewings. A podium stood opposite the camera, and here Mr. Kraft stopped, adopting the pose of grand orator. The members of the school board, faculty, and staff gathered near Kraft, while community guests and the Mesmer Team assembled as an audience.

Sabrina appreciated that her aunts kept a distance—it was hard enough when one's guardians came to campus. Any teenager with any dignity at all hated to be shadowed by adults when peers were watching.

Noisily Kraft cleared his throat. "Good morning, board members and guests. I am Vice-Principal Willard Kraft, and I'm delighted to welcome you to the soon-to-be Willard H. Kraft Learning Center of Westbridge High." He waited for applause. When none came, he plunged on. "This presentation is to be the first of many to come. Inspired by history and dedicated to education, I have always felt that bringing the past into the present was a noble goal. . . ."

Sabrina.

With a startled little jump, Sabrina brought a hand to her forehead.

"Something wrong?" Harvey whispered as Kraft's speech droned on.

"Uh, no," Sabrina told him, but she wasn't sure. Had she just heard Zelda's voice in her head?

That's exactly what you heard, came Zelda's voice again. Sabrina turned to find both her aunts smiling at her. *Calm down, we just cast a short telepathy spell.*

I thought we agreed not to use those, Sabrina thought back.

We don't use them very often, Hilda cut in. *The rates are ridiculously high, especially for a party line like this.*

We just wanted to tell you how proud we are of you, Zelda continued, her thought-voice full of warmth. *You faced an incredible challenge, and you did it all on your own.*

No thanks to you, Sabrina thought to herself, but it automatically got transmitted to Zelda and Hilda.

We'll let that remark go, Hilda thought. *After*

all, using the Oil of Oblivion was our idea, even though it was Zelda who botched it up and made us spend a few days in the Gobi Desert.

The Gobi Desert was your fault, not mine, Zelda thought angrily.

I wouldn't have gone off in a huff if you hadn't messed up the first time, Hilda thought back.

It wasn't all my fault!

It was!

Wasn't!

Was!

Wasn't!

Uh, guys? Sabrina cut in, feeling like her aunts had become as whiny as the Keftiu. *I need to pay attention to Mr. Kraft. You don't get graded for listening to boring speeches, but I do.*

Of course, dear. Zelda blew her a kiss. *We just wanted to apologize and promise never to ignore you again.*

Sabrina grinned wickedly. *Then can I have a car?*

Zelda put a hand to her car. *Did you hear something, Hilda?*

Hilda looked around as if she couldn't see Sabrina anymore. *Not me, Zeldy.*

Hey, you guys are ignoring me again—!

"Sabrina," came Harvey's concerned whisper again, "you sure you're okay?"

"I would be if I could have a car," Sabrina whispered back sourly.

"But this couldn't have happened all by itself," Kraft was droning to his captive audience. "No, aside from my own genius, this is all the result of one man's great generosity. It is my privilege to introduce that man, our benefactor, and a fellow who should be in the *Guinness Book of Records* for the world's longest vacation, Professor Austin Theobald Mesmer."

As everyone applauded, Mesmer stepped forward and gave a short, formal bow. Then he waved at Sabrina and stepped back into place between Zelda and Hilda.

Kraft said of Mesmer, "Thanks to this man, the students of Westbridge High have access to materials and resources that our puny public school budget could never have dreamed of, let alone obtained. With this help, may our school graduate future leaders, future visionaries, and future millionaires who will then donate money to their alma mater!"

At this, the school board, faculty, and staff heartily applauded.

"And now," Kraft continued, "on with our show—a detailed reenactment of Nelson's triumph at Cape Trafalgar!"

The lights dimmed, and from a stereo unit in the corner, Tchaikovsky's *1812 Overture* blared dramatically. The video camera whirred into action, and everyone watched the little model ships floating in the aquarium.

Everyone but Sabrina, that is. She looked at the aquarium, but she wasn't seeing Horatio

Nelson's fleet engage the combined naval strength of the French and Spanish. Instead she was seeing a tranquil miniature city filled with tiny, green flitting forms. *Maybe I* will *visit the Keftiu again some day,* she thought. *After all, being a mermaid is just too cool.*

About the Authors

David Cody Weiss and Bobbi JG Weiss are a hus-
band and wife writing team. They're big fans of
Sabrina, the Teenage Witch and have written a
number of novels for the series including *#3 Good
Switch, Bad Switch*, *#8 Salem on Trial* and *#13 Go
Fetch!* They have also written animation, comic
books and a trilogy of films that never got made!
David and Bobbi live in the USA.

Let Sabrina cast a spell on you in her next magical book . . .

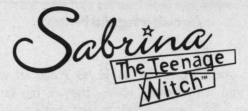

#21 Prom Time
By Bobbi JG Weiss and David Cody Weiss

It's prom time and if Sabrina has her way it's going to be a truly sparkling occasion!

The trouble is snooty Libby's committee queen and the only person she cares about having a good time is . . . herself! It's time for a bit of trickery and Sabrina's soon on the committee too and conjuring up ideas for the most amazing night of the year. One fair wind later and everything's going according to plan . . . or is it? Sabrina certainly hadn't banked on all the crazy consequences her wand waving might have. And it's beginning to seem that this is one dream evening that's likely to turn in to a total nightmare! Ouch!

Don't miss out on any of Sabrina's magical antics —
conjure up a book from the past for a truly
spellbinding read . . .

#16 Now You See Her, Now You Don't
Diana G Gallagher

Whoa! What's going on? Sabrina's doing a disappearing act but
she has no idea how or why. One minute she's in her room up
to her ears in algebra, the next she's in the middle of a novel
or a TV show! Then, a few seconds later — she's back in boring
old reality. So far, no one's spotted her strange
disappearances. But how long can she be that lucky?

It looks like it's another cunning conundrum from the
Quizmaster and Sabrina's going to have to find the solution
fast. She's got a party at the roller rink tonight and if she just
disappears into thin air . . . people might think it's just a teensy
bit odd.

But worse than that, her disappearances are getting more and
more frequent, and each time they last a little bit longer. Is
Sabrina destined to disappear from her own life for good . . .?!

Keep the magic in your life with a sparkling new Sabrina title
out every month!

Nancy Drew™

Another famous detective from Pocket Books

Nancy Drew
Carolyn Keene
Runaway Bride

Nancy Drew
Carolyn Keene
False Pretences

Nancy Drew
Carolyn Keene
Illusions of Evil

Nancy Drew
Carolyn Keene
Making Waves